A SUMMER WITH OUTLAWS

JAMES POWELL

When he was a boy T. G. Shannon loved trains. Now, in 1892, he finally gets to ride them for a living as a messenger on the Missouri, Kansas & Texas line—the "Katy," as it's widely known. Unfortunately, many others are also fascinated by the locomotive, namely the James boys, the Youngers, the Daltons, Bitter Creek Newcomb . . . they rob for a living, and are notorious for it. One moonlit night, masked bandits halt the train, whose mail car contains two safes, a shaky express guard named Hay, and one T.G. Shannon. It's the Daltons!—or so they say. T.G. knows otherwise. In moments, the secret he reveals at the height of the heist forces him into the biggest adventure of his life. A summer with outlaws is about to unfold.

Life with the Clyde and Buster Crosby gang is quite different from what one would expect. Suffice it to say that when they're not planning the next job, gamely fleeing a posse, hiding out in the wilderness, or figuring out what the heck to do with their newest member, they're not doing much, as T.G. soon learns: "Kansas gave me a sage look. 'Well, T.G., that's one thing about this laying low business. Most of the time it's about as much fun as plucking chickens or scalding hogs.'"

Of course for someone new to the outlaw life, someone accustomed to the constraints of his proper family in Coffeyville, Kansas, life with outlaws is an adventure indeed, especially when a gang includes characters like Clyde, Buster, Kansas,

(continued on back flap)

A SUMMER WITH OUTLAWS

JAMES POWELL

WALKER AND COMPANY · NEW YORK

First published in the United States of America in 1984 by the Walker Publishing Company, Inc.

Published simultaneously in Canada by John Wiley & Sons
Canada, Limited, Rexdale, Ontario.

Library of Congress Cataloging in Publication Data

Powell, James.
  A Summer With Outlaws.

  I. Title.
PS3566.0832S8 1984   813'.54   84-15232
ISBN 0-8027-4038-3

Printed in the United States of America

10 9 8 7 6 5 4 3 2 1

For Polly.

CHAPTER 1

PEOPLE remember the James boys, the Youngers, the Daltons, Bill Doolin, Bitter Creek Newcomb, even that hapless group of bunglers called the Jennings gang. Them and more. But just bring up the Clyde and Buster Crosby outfit and see the looks you get. Ask who remembers their youthful, widowed sister — the beautiful Janie Crosby Beaumont. Try to find anything about any of them in a book somewhere, even one specifically on Oklahoma outlaws, or in an old newspaper clipping. A sentence or two, maybe a paragraph, maybe a few confused columns relating to some of their mysterious exploits as a gang, but nothing about them by name, for theirs was purposeful anonymity throughout. You won't locate a thing, believe me.

While you're at it, try to find something about me, too: T. G. Shannon, Jr., messenger for the Pacific Express Company, working in Indian Territory, Kansas, and Texas, in the year 1892. I was only eighteen years old then and claiming twenty-one, when I traveled the Katy (Missouri, Kansas & Texas) railroad in charge of this shipment and that and thought I really was somebody because of all the responsibility I had been given. I thought I was pretty tough, too. I craved excitement, adventure. I wasn't afraid of anybody, even notorious Oklahoma outlaws. I never dreamed I'd not only get held up one night, but kidnapped as well, by one of the gangs. I never dreamed. But it happened. And just you try to find much of anything about it in writing somewhere. Just you try.

Well, there was a brief spate of newspaper stories about it, both when it happened and immediately after all was over. The kidnapping part was unusual enough, I guess; for a while it was even thought it was the Dalton gang who took me. Actually, I knew at the time of the robbery that they weren't the Daltons and said so, with the express guard hiding not twenty feet away to hear me, the minute I saw one of them with his mask off. That dolt of a guard didn't do much to help me that night, but he did hear what I said. In most ways, I'd have been better off without him, even at that.

You see, I figure the one thing that got me into it was the fact that I knew a Dalton when I saw one. Had it not been for that, and had I had the good sense to keep my mouth shut when the shutting was good, I probably never would have spent that summer with outlaws at all.

I was young, and had been known to indulge in what I considered a little innocent bragging about how I had known the Daltons and all when I was growing up around Coffeyville, Kansas, between 1886 and 1890. Truth to tell, I didn't actually *know* those boys—not Bob, Emmett, or Grat. They weren't around Coffeyville much during the years my family was there. The family of Lewis Dalton had come and gone from Montgomery County, Kansas, by the time my pa moved us to those parts, and it wasn't until after U.S. Deputy Marshal Frank Dalton—one of the "good" brothers—was killed late in 1887 that some of that clan moved temporarily back there. Emmett was still pretty young, I guess, but Bob and Grat were grown, and all three were off doing things on their own in Indian Territory and other places at the time. I saw them each several times, though—when they came home for a visit or when their pa died, near Dearing in 1890; I knew well enough what all three looked like—especially the younger two—and when Bob and Emmett eventually took up horse stealing and then train robbery in the territory and started to become famous for it, I was quick to say so.

My own family came originally from eastern Missouri, where I was born nine years after the end of the war between the North and the South. There were nine of us kids in all, six boys and three girls. I came along in the middle of the pack, number five to be exact, and I never knew why my pa waited until his fourth son was born to name one after himself. In addition to three older brothers, I had one older sister and two brothers and two sisters younger than me. At least two of the latter—you know, I can't for the life of me recall for certain whether it was two or three—were born in central Kansas, where we moved when I was five years old. My pa farmed there for seven years, just eking out a living, before moving us farther south to a place near the Verdigris River close to Coffeyville. That was in 1886. Three years later, just before the celebrated opening of the Oklahoma "unassigned lands" in April 1889, my pa was killed when a horse fell on him. He had been thinking about joining the land rush and settling in the new district, but of course his death put a shocking end to all thoughts of that. My oldest brother, Sam, still wanted to give it a try, but the timing of Pa's death and funeral caused him to pass it up—that, and my ma. No sooner had the shock worn off than she was talking of moving the family back to Missouri. She said she almost couldn't stand Kansas as it was, but she definitely couldn't stand it without Pa; she wanted to go home, and she wanted any of her kids who would to go with her.

Well, to make a somewhat involved story as simple as possible, none of us wanted to hurt Ma, but some of us wanted to go and some did not. Sam, the oldest and steadiest of us, and already sporting a wife and two kids of his own, felt more or less obligated, I think. George and Harry, second and third behind Sam, were unmarried and restless and had already been studying on moving away, maybe on west as far as California. Julie, my older sister, was just three months married and had been making plans with her husband to move to Texas. My younger brothers and sisters were too young to do anything but what Ma wanted. And me, I was right at the age— almost sixteen—at which the decision was hardest of all, both for me to make and for Ma to accept.

I didn't care much for farming, and from what I remembered of it, I wasn't that crazy about Missouri, either. I wasn't as old as George or Harry, and I had no craving for California, but I had been thinking for some time about what it would be like to go it on my own. I even had notions about what I would do with myself when it happened. For as long as I could remember, I had been in love with trains, especially those great, noisy monsters that pulled them, the locomotives. I wanted to work on the railroads; I wanted to do something, anything at all, that would allow me to spend most of my time riding the trains.

So I stayed behind, promising to write a letter at least every week and to come and visit whenever I could. I hung around Coffeyville for almost a year, working at this odd job and that, for even though I looked older than my age, I found I was too young to get on with the railroad doing anything much more than cleaning up around the

Coffeyville station house. Besides, folks knew me around Coffeyville; they knew my age. Pretty soon it became evident that I might as well mosey on somewhere else, unless I wanted to wait forever to be old enough to get on with the railroad. Finally, late in 1890, the year the western half of Indian Territory officially became Oklahoma Territory, I made my way the short distance south and east to Vinita in Indian Territory. There I could tell people what I wanted to about my age, and before long I got a job, first as a station agent's helper and later as a day ticket agent for the Katy. It wasn't everything I wanted, but at least it was drawing me closer to it.

In May 1891 the Dalton gang held up their first train in the territories, at Wharton on the Santa Fe, and got away with $1,745 from the Wells Fargo safe. In September, they robbed their first Katy train, at Leliaetta near Wagoner. This time they got off with about $2,500 in silver. Maybe they weren't famous outside Indian Territory yet, but anyone who worked for the railroads or express companies sure had heard of them. It was said that so far only Bob and Emmett, along with some of their pards, were involved.

In April 1892 I was still working at the big station house in Vinita and hadn't been able to find anything actually riding the trains yet when I heard that the express companies were having trouble hiring messengers to man the runs through Indian Territory. Outlaws and robbers were so thick you could stir them like cream. Certain desperate escapades were even getting passed off as those of the Daltons, and only much later was it learned that they really were not. I didn't give a hang about any of that. I only knew I'd give anything to have a job riding one of those trains. The Pacific Express Company took my lie about my age and hired me on two days after I applied.

I did a short training stint riding with other messengers, and then in late May started my own run, on the Katy between Parsons, Kansas, and Dennison, Texas. Indian Territory made up the major share of what lay between the two points.

On the night of June 1, the Dalton gang was credited with a daring robbery of a Santa Fe train twenty-six miles northwest of Wharton at Red Rock. It was rumored that this time older brother Grat (a recent escapee from a California jail) was back with them. For me, it sure was something to be able to brag to the fellows I worked with that I had known those boys back in Coffeyville.

Exactly two weeks after the Red Rock robbery, on Wednesday, June 15, I boarded a Katy southbound at Parsons for my regular run to Dennison. Riding with me was an express guard named Hay. It was the first and last time I rode with this Hay, and I don't to this day remember his first name. It was only my fifth run as a full-fledged messenger, and it was Hay's second as a guard. He was a thin, sallow-faced fellow of about thirty, with a shaky voice and an even shakier look. The only conclusion I could come to about him was that the company must have been in an even worse hurt for guards when they hired him than they were for messengers when they hired me.

In the combination express and mail car with us were two safes— one the company's smaller "local" safe, the other what was called their "through" safe, which ordinarily contained anything of real value such as a bank shipment, mine payroll, or Indian annuity payment. On this run we quickly learned that there was nothing of great value in either safe—a thousand dollars in greenbacks, possibly six hundred in silver, and some nonnegotiable securities. I guess that's why a green messenger and an even greener guard drew the run, proving that express companies weren't totally dumb after all.

Anyway, we left Parsons in time to reach Indian Territory just about dark and Vinita about nine o'clock. After uneventful stops at Adair and Pryor Creek, we took on water at Leliaetta (on which the Daltons had bestowed dubious fame the previous September) and subsequently pulled out for Wagoner and then Muskogee in the Creek Nation.

Wagoner was only four miles down the tracks, and a wayside delivery of freight and mail was scheduled. We did not expect to pick up much speed in the interim, and I was busy getting my small delivery ready, as was the mail clerk in the adjoining compartment. Less than a mile past the Leliaetta water tank, the train suddenly slowed and we heard the low screech of the locomotive's wheels against the steel of the tracks.

Guard Hay looked at me and said, "Now what the hell?"

"We're braking," I said, straightening from my task.

He looked at me as if I was stupid.

The rapid *clunk clunk clunk* of couplings sounded as the train came jarring to a halt; steam hissed. From somewhere outside came a loud, ringing pop, then another. Someone yelled. A horse whinnied. Hay and I exchanged looks, this time apprehensively.

"Oh God," the sallow-faced guard said, his eyes wide. "Oh God."

We were both armed with shotguns, and I said, "Look, Hay, this is why we've got jobs here. You especially. Let's not lose our grip on things before we're even sure what's happening."

"It's train robbers," he said, almost as if choking. "My God! At Leliaetta again! Just like last fall! Didn't you hear about it? The Daltons held up a Katy express right here last fall!"

Another shot rang out, this time ricocheting off steel with a loud *spang* and whistling off into the night. It had come from very close by. Trying to remain calm despite the quaking guard at my side, I quickly checked the padlock on the side door and blew out the lights inside the compartment. As I felt for my shotgun, left propped against one of the safes, I heard the guard go stumbling forward, muttering about trying to see outside. He probably had forgotten all about his own shotgun as he approached the narrow-paned glass of the express car side door (our only way of seeing out), and I could just see his head and shoulders outlined against the glass as he looked out.

"I see 'em! Oh God, I see 'em out there!"

"Who?"

"Hell, I don't know. Four men . . . One of 'em's the engineer and another's the stoker. Oh God!"

I was getting pretty tired of hearing "Oh God" all over the place, but I didn't feel the leisure of worrying long over something like that. As nervous as the guard was, I figured he knew what he was talking about. There was a full moon out that night; the seeing was good enough. And I'd heard enough about train robberies to know the pattern. However the robbers got the train stopped—there were different ways, of course—the next step was to capture the engineer and the fireman and, mostly in order to keep these two out of mischief while the robbery was going on, march them back to the express car. In our case, this wasn't much of a march, for we were the next thing behind the tender. Behind us was a smoker, a Pullman, two coach cars, and a caboose. Depending on how many robbers were involved, someone would handle the business at the express car while others kept watch on and possibly even robbed the passengers. The procedure didn't vary much. Sometimes the robbers did a lot of shooting to scare the passengers; sometimes they were frightfully quiet. That was about the size of it. Train robbery was a pretty well-refined art by 1892.

A loud pounding on the express car door caused me to jump and Guard Hay to stumble back among some boxes stacked toward the back of the car. "Open up in there! Now!"

I hefted my shotgun and stepped well back from the door, taking care not to trip and fall down in the dark. I didn't say a word.

"Hey in there! Can't you hear?"

Finally I said, "I can hear. What do you want?"

"We want in, you idiot!"

It was a harsh voice, certainly not that of the engineer or fireman. "Well, I'm not going to let you in," I said, trying to summon the needed determination.

I heard a sharp curse and then words I couldn't understand. Presently a new voice was heard. "This is the engineer, son. Please, I think you're going to have to do as he says. He has a gun at my head, and they've got dynamite. They say they'll blow us all to smithereens if you don't let them in."

From way in the back of the car somewhere — probably hidden behind the boxes — Guard Hay begged, "For chrissakes, kid, do as he says! What's in that safe ain't worth it. Open the door and let 'em have what they want!"

And then from outside, a new voice hollered, "Hey, Bob, Emmett — what's the holdup?" Guard Hay groaned aloud and said, "Oh God," and I very slowly laid my shotgun aside and with unsteady fingers unlocked the padlock to the express car door.

"Fire up a light in there," one of several dark figures on the ground outside ordered harshly.

Obediently I found my way over to a lamp and lit it. As I turned back to the door, a man in a dark coat and hat and wearing a blue bandanna over his face scrambled up inside the car and stood covering me with a huge-looking Colt Peacemaker. A second man, dressed almost identically to the first, followed close behind. I could just make out a third masked man still outside, sitting astride a dark-colored horse and holding a gun on the engineer and fireman.

"Okay, Emmett, get his shotgun," the first robber ordered.

"Sure, Bob," the second answered, and I was already wondering at this undisciplined use of given names when he said to me, "Hands up, there. Are you the messenger? Is there a guard in here?"

I glanced around. "I'm the messenger," I said, then added in a somewhat sarcastic voice that I was sure Hay would hear, "Do you see anyone else?"

"Don't get smart," he told me as he checked me out for a sidearm.

"Better mind what he says," came the voice of the engineer from outside. "I think these men are the Daltons."

I tried to look into the eyes of the one calling himself Bob, but he wouldn't fully meet my gaze. He was blue-eyed like Bob Dalton; I could tell no more than that.

"Enough gab," he said gruffly. "The safes, messenger; we want in those safes. And don't give me any nonsense about not knowing the combination to the through safe. We know you do."

It was pretty standard for messengers to try telling train robbers that the combination to the through safe had been wired ahead to its contents' destination but had been withheld from the messenger. This was supposedly done to make it impossible for him to open it on just such an occasion as I now faced. Some outlaws, it would seem, knew better than to accept the routine.

"If you knew anything at all," I said, bending to open the local safe first, "you wouldn't be wasting your time on what's inside either one of these. You're sure gonna be disappointed."

"Just open 'em and shut up," the one called Bob barked.

I did as I was told and stepped back to let them see for themselves. The one they referred to as Emmett produced a burlap sack from beneath his coat and began to rifle the safes, the big one first. "Damn," he said. "He wasn't far wrong. You couldn't spend a lot of this stuff anywhere, but at least there's some silver."

Suddenly there was a shot from outside, farther back along the train. This was followed by maybe half a dozen shots from different weapons, all coming in short order. The one called Bob whirled around to look out the door, and as he did his mask fell. He was in the light, and I got as good a look at him as one could expect to get. Almost instinctively I blurted out, "Why, you're not Bob Dalton! You don't look anything like him!" I looked at "Emmett." "I know what Bob Dalton looks like as good as anybody. You fellows are imposters!"

Both men glared at me as if they'd love to have choked me, and

"Bob" quickly jerked the mask back over his nose. More shots reverberated outside and the man on the horse yelled, "Hurry up, dammit! Something's breaking loose back around the coaches."

"Bob" and "Emmett" were still looking at me. They exchanged glances. "Do you think the engineer or fireman heard what he said?"

"I don't think so."

"Bob" said to me, "You say another word and I'll plug you, you hear?" Then, after a moment's indecision, he said to his companion, "We're taking him with us. If he says anything to anybody, shoot him."

"Emmett" looked almost as surprised as I was. But then there was more shooting and he stuck a gun in my ribs and said, "Come on; you heard him. You're going with us."

Because I didn't want to wear a permanent hole in my side, I did as he said. Way back in the express car, still hiding behind a stack of boxes, Guard Hay quaked in his shoes and didn't do a solitary thing to help me.

CHAPTER 2

IT took only a few moments for my eyes to adjust to the darkness as I jumped to the ground outside. The engineer and fireman stood harmlessly back against the express car, while a robber on horseback fired his pistol in the air nearby. Two more riders came pounding up, each leading a saddled horse. The one calling himself Bob glanced at me, then said to one of the riders, "Janie, give this speck of dust your horse and get on behind me. And you, messenger, no less than four guns will be on you, so just come along and don't try anything."

A slight figure dismounted quickly, and I was ushered onto his horse. I wondered at the name Janie and looked quickly over at the engineer and fireman to see if either of them had heard. They gave no sign that they had. I felt a gun at my side again as "Emmett" rode up beside me. "Follow the horse ahead of you. I'll be right behind. Don't forget that."

We charged off into the moonlit night, around and in front of the still-chuffing locomotive and across the tracks. Guns continued to fire sporadically behind us for a minute or so, but of course uselessly. Voices—yells and screams—faded behind us. The lights of Wagoner were to our left, those of a farmhouse to our right. Then we were in darkness, with only the moon to light our way. We must have gone at least four miles before stopping. When we finally did pull up, it was within a creek-bottom grove of tall ash or cottonwood trees, to stop and "check out the loot and divvy up"—in case, I gathered, the train robbers should be forced to split up unexpectedly later on.

The pause came none too soon for me, for the stirrups on the saddle I was riding were far too short for me to sit comfortably, and I welcomed the chance to stop and lengthen them. Still, I dismounted only after "Emmett" had tossed the burlap bag filled with booty on the ground and told me to get down.

"Somebody build a fire," one of them said. "Let's see what we got."

The horses were tied, and I was shoved roughly over toward where the fire was already being built. "What're we gonna do with him, Clyde?" one of them asked, addressing the one previously referred to as Bob.

"I dunno yet. Just sit him down and keep an eye on him. Later, we'll decide."

I was plopped down hard on the ground and told to stay there, which I didn't figure I had any choice but to do. Pretty soon a low fire was crackling and four of the robbers sat immediately around it. I sat back a ways from them. All had removed their masks by now, and the fifth member of the gang proved to be a girl, the one they called Janie. She sat only a few feet from me, and seemed both young and pretty. She was so pretty, in fact, I guess I got caught staring at her without even realizing that's what I had been doing. Of course, it had to be the girl herself who caught me doing it.

She seemed almost uninterested as she watched her companions empty the contents of the burlap sack on a blanket, then gather around to count it out. She sat with her revolver in her lap and her attention more on me than I had realized. The firelight gave me a good view of her.

"You find me interesting, do you?" She seemed amused.

Before, she had been wearing a dark-colored hat like the rest of the gang, but now she discarded it. From beneath the hat tumbled a mass of light brown hair and in the firelight I could see that her eyes were quite blue. Her features were even and her complexion, though tanned beneath the hatline on her forehead, seemed smooth. Her clothing (a man's or boy's coat, shirt, and trousers) did much to hide her figure, which I suspected was more girlish than womanish. Certainly it was not boyish.

"Well," she said, smiling, "are you going to answer me, or did my brother Clyde scare the talk right out of you?"

"I'm sorry," I finally managed. "I didn't mean to be rude. But no, I'm not scared of your brother Clyde. Not at all."

She continued to look amused, and although I don't think she could have been a day older than I was, her demeanor almost made me feel like a child. "You aren't worried about what he's going to do with you?" she asked.

I shrugged. "Maybe a little. But I figure that now that you folks are on the run, I'm just so much baggage. Seems to me the only smart thing for him to do in that light is to just let me go."

Suddenly she didn't seem amused anymore. "Why did he take you? I mean, do you know?"

At first I was a little surprised at this, but then I thought, Of course it was possible that she would not know. She hadn't been anywhere near when that discussion had taken place, and there had been little real opportunity for explanation since.

"Well, I reckon it was because he and these other fellows were pretending to be the Dalton gang, and I let on that I knew they weren't. Your brother didn't seem to like that very much."

"You knew they weren't the Daltons? You really *knew* that?"

"Your brother's mask slipped," I explained. "Anyone who's ever seen Bob Dalton would know it wasn't him."

"You've *seen* Bob Dalton? You *know* him?"

I squirmed a little before answering, but wound up once again letting my pride get the better of me. "Sure, I know him. Him and Emmett, even Grat. I know them all. Sure, I do."

She eyed me skeptically. "From where? When?"

"Why, Coffeyville, Kansas. I lived there for a while, and so did they. They were U.S. deputy marshals or possemen, all of them, just like their brother Frank, who was killed. I used to see them all the time . . . "

Something told me I'd just made a mistake—not only in saying this but in saying it too loudly—when like lightning the activity around the blanket ceased and all eyes were suddenly on me, especially brother Clyde's. He said, "That's interesting, messenger, damned interesting. Isn't it, boys?"

"Aw, come on, Clyde," the one who had previously been called Emmett said. "Forget him. We never should have taken him in the first place. It was a dumb thing to do. We should have just shot him."

"Shut up, Buster. You know my policy on that." (I was wishing *I* knew.)

Buster looked hurt. "Well, dammit, you asked."

Clyde ignored him this time. "Tell me, messenger, did you know any other Daltons besides those you mentioned? Are there any other brothers?"

"Well," I said, hesitating only because I knew I was being tested, "there is one named Bill, I think. And a Ben, and one they call Lit. But I never knew any of them. They were gone from home and this part of the country by the time I was in Coffeyville."

"And their pa? What's his name?"

"Lewis, I think. But he's dead. They buried him near Dearing a couple of years ago. The family's moved away again now."

He bobbed his head thoughtfully and said again, "Interesting. We might just could use you." He looked past me to the girl. "Keep an eye on him, Janie." Then he started to turn back to the blanket and the business at hand.

"Wait a minute," I said. "What do you mean, use me? What are you going to do with me? Why did you take me like this?"

He turned back very deliberately and for a moment just stared at me. "We took you, you flaming idiot, because you talk too much. I don't know yet what we'll do with you." And then he grinned. "But don't worry. Even if we decide to shoot you, we'll tell you when it's time."

They all laughed at that, everyone except maybe the girl—and me, of course. The boys went back to dividing up their loot.

I looked at the girl. "I guess he's right, isn't he?"

"In what way?" she asked, sort of scooting herself around so that she could sit more or less facing me. She also achieved a slightly greater distance from me than before.

"That I talk too much. I guess I do, don't I?"

"I would say that's possible, yes." She smiled, but I noticed that her hand had not left the revolver in her lap. I found myself staring at that revolver.

"What's the matter?" she asked. "Are you wondering if I can use this?"

"Well, I suppose I was wondering if you *would* use it."

She smiled once more. It was an awfully pretty smile. Disarming. "You wouldn't expect me to say no to that, would you?"

"No . . . I suppose not."

"Well, let's just say don't do anything to make us find out for sure, okay?"

The outlaws weren't as unhappy with their take as I had thought they would be. Not that they were all that ecstatic about it either, but at least they seemed to take it in stride that the haul was a light one.

They threw all the nonnegotiables in the fire, jammed their shares of the good stuff in money belts (Clyde seemed to be the treasurer for three of the shares and the keeper of two of them), and they were finished. In all, no more than thirty minutes were needed for the entire money-counting operation.

Presently dirt was kicked over the fire and we were back on our horses, crossing a creek and heading out in what I decided was a westerly direction. The moon was high overhead and my pocket watch registered almost midnight. Clyde and Janie, riding double, led the way, and I came along right behind them. The other three followed me in a bunch, sort of like they were herding me, and despite whatever Clyde's policy on killing was, I had no doubt that had I made any attempt to break from the pack they would have gunned me down instantly. Well, I had *some* doubt, but not enough to risk challenging them. I might talk too much at times, but I wasn't wholly stupid.

I guess some might consider it exciting, romantic, that moonlight ride of mine in the company of outlaws. I might too — if I hadn't been there. Mostly it was a pain. Twice before dawn we forded major rivers, first the Verdigris and then the Arkansas. Especially in the latter, I got wet from the waist down; and because I wasn't really accustomed to riding that much or that hard, my legs were soon rubbed raw to the point of real misery. As we slanted northwest following the rich bottomlands of the Arkansas, my main memory is of being bone-tired, sore, and sleepy. In fact, I had about decided I couldn't go any farther when just at dawn we finally rode beneath long, twin lines of trees up to the farmhouse of a half-blood Creek Indian somewhere south of Bixby, where the gang seemed to think we were going to take a respite.

Clyde appeared to know the Indian (I never did catch the man's name), and it soon became clear we were going to be put up in his barn, perhaps for the day. I guess this last part was especially important to the gang, because our horses were pretty well used up, and who could say how many posses would soon be scouring the countryside hoping to bring us to ground?

The barn was big and dark and smelled of harness leather and horses. The Indian seemed a little nervous, as if he was afraid of Clyde, as he showed us where to bed down and then went on back up to the house. Before he left, however, he got Clyde to promise that if anyone discovered us there we would say we had sneaked in during the night and that the owner had no knowledge of our presence. Clyde watched him leave the barn, then turned to Buster and grinned. "Dumb half-breed."

We slept in horse stalls on musty-smelling hay and without the need for bedrolls (although everyone except me had one), and because of my prisoner status I was tied hand and foot before being allowed to turn in. It wasn't very comfortable, but I was so bushed I really didn't care. I fell asleep almost instantly.

I don't remember exactly when I learned all of their names and what little I ever knew about their backgrounds. That came a little here and a little there, I guess. Mostly it was later on, but now seems as good a time as any to describe them to you.

Clyde and Buster were brothers, and it seems that Crosby was their real name and not an alias. Clearly Clyde was the leader of the gang. He was of medium height, somewhat husky of build, blue-eyed, and fair. He wore his dirty-blond hair moderately long, and perhaps his only really bad physical feature was a set of moderately prominent buck teeth. I don't know if you would class him as especially intelligent, but at least he was a pretty cagey thinker. He was, that summer of 1892, twenty-four years old.

Brother Buster, on the other hand, was only twenty-one, and there was very little resemblance between the two. Where Clyde was stocky, Buster was built about like a nail with arms and legs. Where Clyde was fair, Buster was dark of both hair and eyes. Where Clyde could be classed as cagey and possibly even innovative, Buster tended toward passive thinking. They had been born and reared in Texas and had been roaming around Oklahoma and Indian territories for only about a year. That had been long enough for them to involve themselves in several small-time robberies of various sorts, but the holdup of my Katy train was their first of real consequence. It was also the first in which the idea of impersonating the Daltons had been put to use. This tactic was Clyde's invention from beginning to end.

The other two men in the gang were no relation to the Crosbys. Kansas Jim McDay (called almost exclusively Kansas by the gang) was easily the oldest member of the bunch — twenty-eight — and was the only one ever to have been a cowboy. He had also been a horse

thief, a cow thief, and a general ne'er-do-well for the better part of his
adult years. Also a Texan, he had never set foot in Kansas in his life.
He like the sound of the name, however—an alias from beginning to
end—and was unbothered by its complete lack of authenticity. As an
outlaw, he may not have been quite in the class of the Jameses, the
Youngers, the Daltons, or Bill Doolin, but he was not the sort to be
taken lightly, either.

Juice Ledoux was the fourth man in the gang, one year younger
than Clyde Crosby. I don't think I ever saw such a homely man. He
was also short, possibly reaching no more than two inches over five
feet, and what caused him to aspire seriously to become an outlaw I
never really knew. The one thing that might have gotten him in with
the Crosbys was his claim that he knew Bill Doolin, who was at the
time reputed to be running with the Daltons and later made a name
for himself as the leader of his own gang. I never knew whether
Juice's claim was true or not.

And then there was Janie. Janie Crosby Beaumont, eighteen
years old and already a widow—the prettiest human female I believe
I ever knew. Her you better get acquainted with the same way I did.
She very definitely was the most remarkable member of the outlaw
gang.

When I awoke, there in that Indian's horse stall, it was not only to
pain and stiffness in my back and legs and arms, but to an enormous
pressure from inside my bladder. As if that and being tied hand and
foot weren't bad enough, the first and only person I saw upon
waking was the girl. She was standing just outside my horse stall,
and I felt that she had been watching me. Afternoon sunlight
streamed in through an open loft window on the west side of the
barn.

The expression on the girl's face was one of at least mild sympathy. "You look pretty uncomfortable, all tied up that way."

"You only know the half of it," I groaned, trying to sit up.

"The boys are all still asleep," she advised matter-of-factly. "Try
not to wake them up, okay?"

I looked at her. Without the coat she had worn the night before,
even the shirt, trousers, and man-sized revolver carried holstered at
her hip did little to diminish her clearly feminine shape.

"I couldn't sleep any longer," she explained. "I'm not much on
sleeping in daytime. I don't guess you are either."

I looked around, half in desperation. "Look, miss, it's not that. It's
. . . I mean, I, uh, need to . . ."

Understanding shone at once in her eyes, and she seemed to
suppress a laugh. "There's a privy out behind the main house. If you
want, I'll untie you and take you there."

I gawked at her. "*Take* me there? Now, look, miss—I don't need
anyone to escort me to the privy, especially not some girl!"

This time she did laugh. "I'm sorry, but I can't let you go
anywhere alone. You might try to get away, and Clyde would have
my hide if you did that."

I looked at her as balefully as I knew how.

"Oh, come on, it won't be so bad. I won't actually go in with you.
I'll wait outside at a respectable distance. You'll see."

"No," I said stubbornly.

"Well, suit yourself," she said with a shrug. "I guess there's always
your horse stall, or maybe you could just wait until one of the boys
wakes up—"

"No!" I said emphatically. But as she shrugged again and started
to turn away, I called after her. "Wait a minute . . . Can't we wake
one of the boys up now? I mean . . ."

She turned back. "Oh, I don't think you'd want to do that. The
boys were all pretty tired last night. And they get awfully grumpy
when they're rousted out before they're ready to get up. No, I don't
think we should do that."

I wondered if she was enjoying this. I said, "Okay, okay, for Pete's
sake. Untie me. You can even go in with me, I don't care!"

She laughed again as she bent first to untie my feet, then had me
turn so that she could release my hands. She stood back as I rubbed
the numbness out of my arms and tried to stretch a few badly
abused muscles. Very slowly I got to my feet. She pointed to the
barn door and said, "Just remember, I have my gun here. Don't do
anything stupid."

"Don't worry," I said. "I couldn't run if I wanted to right now."

We left the barn and entered the bright sunlight of early afternoon. For a few seconds I just stood squinting at the house—a low,
hand-hewn log structure located about fifty yards from the barn.
The privy was twenty or so paces to the rear of the house. No one
was in evidence around the place, but I felt quite uncomfortable
with the situation anyway. "I hope to God nobody sees this," I said,
starting to walk on stiff legs in the direction of the privy.

"Don't fret," she said. "They've all had to go there themselves at one time or another. They'll understand."

"Doesn't it bother you that no one seems to be around?" I asked as we walked.

"Well," she said thoughtfully, "I don't know."

I stood for a moment at the privy door, looking back at her. True to her word, she had stopped a respectable distance away and was simply waiting. I noticed, however, that her attention seemed divided between me and the grounds around the house, her expression possibly just the slightest bit worried. I went inside, and when I reemerged a couple of minutes later, she still stood there with that same expression on her face.

"What's the matter?" I asked.

"You were right. Something's wrong. I think the Indian has taken his family and pulled out."

"Which means?"

"I'm not sure. But come on. Let's get back to the barn."

I led the way again, and we were almost at the barn door when the girl suddenly said, "Oh-oh."

I looked back. Her gaze was directed up the lane leading to the house. It was almost completely shaded by the trees lining either side. A group of riders had just come dimly into view at the far end of the lane.

"Get inside," she told me. "Come on, hurry!"

Inside, she called out in the direction of the horse stalls, "Clyde! Buster! Shake out of there quick! I think we've got trouble outside."

CHAPTER 3

I never saw four previously sleeping men move as quickly into action as those four did just then. All were tousle-haired and red-eyed and had straw poking out from their clothes and hair, but they were up and charging around almost instantly.

"What is it?" Clyde already had his revolver in hand as he strode toward his sister and me. He was followed closely by the other three men.

"I think your Indian friend sold us out," the girl told him. "I don't see any sign of him or his family around the place, and I just spotted a bunch of riders coming up the lane. They look like a posse to me."

Clyde cracked the door just enough to see out, then breathed an oath.

"What is it? What are they doing?" Brother Buster asked from over his shoulder.

"They're not doing anything right now. They've stopped about halfway up the lane, just sitting there." He watched for a moment more, then drew away and said, "Juice, Kansas—get the horses. Buster, you help them saddle up." And glancing at me he said to the girl, "What the hell is he doing untied?"

"He needed to take a walk to the privy," she explained. "We never would have seen the posse or noticed the Indian gone if it hadn't been for that."

He gave me one of those even-flies-have-some-purpose looks and said, "Okay, but you keep an eye on him, you hear? He's your responsibility till we get out of this, and I don't want any messing up."

She seemed almost amused. "Sure, Clyde. I can handle it."

The night before, our horses had been saddled, grained, and

turned loose in a small corral behind the barn. Fortunately, this was opposite the side facing the lane and the posse. Buster, Juice, and Kansas were already leading three of the horses inside and Kansas was apparently thinking ahead about the situation with the mounts.

"Hey, Clyde," he called out. "That Indian has a couple of nags out back. You want us to catch one for the messenger? Your horse ain't gonna last long if you and Janie keep riding him double the way you did last night."

Clyde never took his eye away from the crack in the doorway. "If you can find a saddle to go with the nag, yeah, hell, I guess so." Among other things, I think he was beginning to wish he had never seen me.

"What are they doing now, Clyde?" Janie asked presently.

"I'm not sure. They haven't come any closer; I think they're trying to figure some way to spread out and surround us."

Through a knothole in one of the wall planks I too managed to look out. Other than the long lines of trees on either side of the road, open fields claimed the scene. But as anyone who had just viewed things from the house and the privy would know, things were different behind the barn. There, thick woods covered a low group of hills leading up and away from the valley. The posse, perhaps belatedly realizing that they were approaching from the wrong direction, were now faced with the problem of how to get around and behind us before we detected their presence and managed to take to the woods ahead of them. Our problem would seem to lie in not letting them do that.

I think all of this occurred to Clyde about the same time it did me, for he turned suddenly and said, "Janie, you and the messenger get back there and help saddle horses. If we scoot on out of here, I think we've got a chance to avoid a fight."

Across the barn, Buster already had two horses saddled and Kansas and Juice were leading in three more. Kansas dumped a saddle and a blanket that he had found somewhere at my feet. "That's yours, messenger. Throw it on this bay nag here."

I proceeded to do as I was told, adjusting the stirrups in the process, and presently we had six horses saddled and ready to go. Clyde took one more look through the crack in the door. "They're coming now. They probably don't know they've been seen, or at least they don't care. About half of them have spread out on either side of the land, and I'm sure they'll be trying to get behind us." He strode rapidly toward us. "It's now or never, so let's go!"

We led our horses into the corral in back of the barn and through a gate beyond the corral, where we quickly mounted. My horse, the only truly fresh mount, crow-hopped around with me a bit, but I guess he was too dumb to realize that I was not the best of riders, for he gave up almost before he had begun.

Kansas rode past me and said, "You're a horse thief now, messenger. How does it feel?"

Naturally I didn't think it felt too good, but I saw no sense in saying so. Besides, there was no time. Scarcely had we lined out behind Clyde in the direction of the nearest trees when several shots rang out behind us. Juice Ledoux gave a painful yelp and a curse, and Clyde gave his horse the spur. More shots were fired, causing the rest of us to follow suit. In the process there was some confusion, and I guess that was the time when I could have broken loose and turned back. But I didn't. That posse gave no sign of being able to tell a kidnapped express messenger from just another outlaw. The shots they were firing were meant just as much for me as for anyone else.

"I'm shot in the foot, dammit!" Juice yelled as we rode. "Dammit, I'm shot!"

We reached the woods and promptly pulled up to see what the score was behind us. Apparently one flanking group of possemen had moved out far enough to catch sight of us around one corner of the barn, and it was they who had done the firing. They were still a couple hundred yards away, riding through the Indian's field, and Clyde seemed to think a few well-aimed shots from our end would be appropriate to slow them down a bit.

Three outlaw rifles were produced as if by magic, and a couple of rapid volleys certainly did scatter those possemen. Only Juice and the girl refrained from the firing—he because of the sudden preoccupation with his wounded foot, and she because of a preoccupation of her own with keeping both an eye and a revolver on me.

"Don't forget, messenger," the girl said. "I promised Clyde no mistakes where you're concerned."

"Look," I said. "I'm just hoping not to get shot by that posse back there. I'm darn sure not going to do anything to make you shoot me."

"You are very wise," she said.

More shots resounded, this time coming from a second group of riders who were attempting to flank us from the other side of the barn. The boys released another set of volleys, and once again possemen ducked for cover.

"Let's go," Clyde said. "We can't let that second bunch get around us in these trees. Stick together and stick to the woods. Come on!"

It was a hell of a ride, through the trees and across deep gullies and creek bottoms. But thanks to the woods, we never caught sight of our pursuers (nor apparently they us) again. All along, however, Juice kept complaining about his foot, and finally we felt it safe to stop and check on it.

"You're gonna be a cripple," Kansas announced, following a quick inspection, during which only he and Clyde had dismounted.

"Maybe this'll keep you from bleeding to death, though," Clyde told him as they cut Juice's boot away and wrapped the injured foot tightly with their bandannas.

We stayed with the trees until it seemed prudent to reenter the valley, within an hour of sundown. There were a few scattered farmhouses to be seen, but Clyde very carefully avoided these. We followed the Arkansas until along about dark we reached a point where the river began to curve mostly north, in the direction of Tulsa. We continued on to the northwest, and once again left the valley.

"We'll stop to fix up something to eat and rest the horses just as soon as we find a good place," Clyde told us. "But we'll have to ride on through the night after that. That posse was just timid enough to lose us in the woods, but that doesn't mean they'll quit. Someone among those farms back there will have seen us, and if the posse picks up our trail again, we had better be long gone from here."

"Long gone to where, Clyde?" Kansas wanted to know. "The Triangle country—is that still it?"

I perked up immediately at this. I had heard of the "Triangle" many times—that wild and rugged piece of outlaw haven situated between the Arkansas and the Cimarron rivers in the extreme eastern portion of the Cherokee Strip. It was bounded on the south by the Creek Nation, on the north by the Osages, and on the west by the Pawnees. Heavily wooded and pinched to a point on the east by the junction of the two rivers, it was perhaps as good a place to get lost in as Oklahoma had to offer, and apparently the gang had already made plans to go there. The only problem, according to Clyde, was that it could not be reached in a single night's ride.

"I figure we'll cross the Arkansas tonight, somewhere west of Tulsa. Tomorrow we'll hide out across the river and tomorrow night make our way on up through Osage country in the direction of the Triangle. Anybody disagree with that?"

Nobody said anything, except Juice, who moaned, "I just wish to God we'd stop so I can tend to my foot. I could lose the damned thing, you know."

"I know," Clyde said. "I know."

Kansas rode up beside Clyde. "We were lucky back there, Crosby. You know that, don't you?"

"Yeah, I know it," Clyde muttered. "And if I ever see that Creek half-blood again, I sure am gonna repay him for his hospitality. Boy, am I ever gonna do that!"

What we didn't know at the time was that about half the law-enforcement community of Oklahoma and Indian territories was spread out far to the west of us in a desperation manhunt for the Dalton gang. That Red Rock train robbery of theirs was now just two weeks old, and although initial reports had attributed the robbery of my own express car on the Katy to them, that bit of misinformation had not yet become widespread. In the case of the Crosbys' job, confusion reigned. Even the doubters of those early reports could not guess who the robbers really were — not even that Creek half-blood knew Clyde by his right name — and except for the one posse who had attacked us, fewer yet seemed at the moment to care. I am now convinced that we got away, across the Arkansas in the direction of the Osage reservation, largely because of that. The posse chasing us had, in fact, been led by a U.S. deputy marshal, but they were distracted a short distance north of Bixby by near-hysterical reports that the Daltons — other members of the fast-moving gang the posse had just lost, perhaps — were now on the Sac and Fox reservation to the west of us, preparing for another strike against the railroad. I don't know whether these reports were true or not, but I figure it effectively took the heat off us, at least for the time being.

As I say, we did not know any of this at the time. We had every reason to believe the posse would still pick up our thinly disguised trail. They might even enlist Indian police to help them track us.

So it was another of those night rides. Hard on the horses, hard on us. I didn't even know where we were most of the time, except when we finally crossed the Arkansas west of Tulsa, and I wasn't very sure even then. A moonlit hour before daybreak we entered a creek bottom that was really a sizeable canyon. It was overgrown with brush and trees and contained a cave, its mouth fifteen feet across and overlooking an open area between it, the creek, and the only slightly more distant breaks of the river. We staked our horses out to graze and took up hiding for the day.

At least that's what some of us did. Clyde seemed to think we were safe enough there, but Juice's foot was driving the little man to the point of near frenzy. Clearly now, the need for medical care could no longer be ignored. When Clyde and Kansas took Juice down to the creek to bathe and soak the wound, they found that the bullet had entered the inside part of his heel and had torn through to exit at the fleshy, outside part of his foot. He must have been spurring to high heaven when it happened, for the projectile to have caught him at such an angle. On their way back from the creek, Kansas tried to console him by telling him that no major bones were smashed, and better yet, his horse had not been hit in the process. Juice's discomfort was not much eased by this.

Clyde told us, "We're gonna have to get him to a doctor. I think I know where I can find one we can trust, but it's no good for all of us to go. We look too suspicious in a bunch, and I don't want the messenger getting someplace he can shoot his mouth off." He turned to Juice, who had collapsed to a sitting position at the mouth of the cave and was just staring at his bloody-bandaged foot. "Do you think you can stand another ride, Juice?"

Juice allowed sourly that his foot's chances seemed slim at best, none if he couldn't, and Clyde turned to Buster. "We're going to need some grub and stuff anyway, so the trip won't just be for Juice's foot. Kansas and I will go with him. I don't reckon you and Janie will mind staying here and keeping watch on the messenger, will you?"

Buster watched Kansas stalk off to resaddle their horses, then said, "Well, I guess I don't mind staying behind, but this messenger —what are we finally gonna *do* with him?"

"I haven't decided yet about that," Clyde said. "Except we can't just turn him loose. You just keep an eye on him, you hear?"

"When will you be back?" Janie wanted to know.

"That's hard to say. Could be sometime tonight; could be tomorrow or later. It just depends on what the doc can do for Juice. I guess if we're not here by sundown tomorrow, though, you three had better head on for the Triangle. Buster can find the way. We'll just have to meet you there."

A few minutes later Clyde, Kansas, and Juice mounted still-tired horses and proceeded to ride off toward the river breaks. It was barely sunup by then, and when the three of them were out of sight, Buster turned and said, "Well, no use us just standing here. What say we get a little shut-eye while we've got the chance?"

I looked from one to the other of them. "I guess that means I'll have to be tied up again."

"I reckon them's the breaks, all right," Buster allowed.

"It sure would be nice if there was some other way, though," I persisted.

He turned and gave me a suspicious look. "Yeah? Like what?"

I just shrugged my obvious thought on that, and Janie said to Buster, "It *is* pretty uncomfortable for him." Then she turned to me. "I'm sorry, messenger. You seem like a nice young man and probably don't deserve what we're doing to you. I really wish there was some other way."

"Maybe you could just tell Clyde I got away while you and Buster were sleeping. He'd never know the difference, and I'd be out of your hair for good. Then everybody would be happier."

I really think Buster was sorely tempted by this, but the girl gave my suggestion almost no thought at all. "I'm sorry, but no. Clyde would never buy that. And besides, he's our brother. We're all in this together, and Clyde's the one who knows best what to do. We never lie to Clyde."

I just stared at her, wondering if she was serious. She didn't seem the kind to exhibit such blind allegiance—even to her own brother. Nevertheless, I finally decided that maybe, at least in the case of Clyde, I was wrong.

"Still," she went on thoughtfully, "maybe we don't actually have to tie anybody up. We could take turns watching him, Buster. I'm not sleepy right now, anyway. Why don't I watch for a spell, then after a while I'll wake you up so you can watch while I sleep. I'll even make a pot of coffee for when you wake up, both of you."

Buster seemed hesitant. "Well, I don't know . . ."

"Oh, come on," the girl said. "It'll work, won't it, messenger? You won't try anything, will you?" She patted the revolver at her side, and I just nodded tiredly in the affirmative. I figured I had a right to lie a little bit, just in case my chance did come.

Finally Buster said okay and pointed me toward the cave. I took my saddle and saddle blanket, found a spot that looked not only reasonably clean but *sans* spiders and snakes, and spread the blanket out where I could lie on it. Buster tossed his bedroll a few feet away, between me and the mouth of the cave, while Janie produced a coffeepot from somewhere and busied herself collecting firewood. I don't know who fell asleep first, me or Buster; I never heard him snore.

All I know is, when I next awoke the sun was high overhead and Buster was snoring loudly nearby. The smell of fully brewed coffee drifted my way, and in front of the cave Janie sat beside the fire she had built, her head resting on her arms, which were folded atop her updrawn knees. I lay very still until I was convinced that she, too, had fallen fast asleep.

CHAPTER 4

I lay there for a minute longer, pondering my chances and trying to think ahead to what I would do if I actually did make my escape. I tried to catch sight of the horses staked nearby, but the lip of the cave floor and the girl hid them from my view. All I could really see were the sky, a tip edge of the sun, and the tops of some rather tall cottonwoods down by the creek. From somewhere birds were chirping and one of the horses cleared its nostrils. Buster still snored and Janie had not moved.

I determined that if I could get by the girl, my next priority must then be the horses. I looked around thoughtfully. My bay's bridle still lay outside the cave and could be easily reached, but I knew I couldn't risk dragging a saddle down there; it would be too cumbersome and the risk of making noise far too great. I would have to ride bareback. I also doubted that I could get away with trying to steal a gun. Buster had both rifle and revolver at his side and Janie's only weapon seemed to be the six-gun in her holster. My only hope was to slip away quietly and put all the distance I could between them and me before they realized I was gone.

Very slowly I rose to a sitting position. Neither Buster nor Janie stirred. I removed my shoes and stood up. Barefoot, I figured I could tiptoe right past both of them and on down the slope to the horses. Carrying my shoes like a wayward husband sneaking in from a night on the town, I left the cave and slipped past the sleeping girl. I picked up the bay's bridle and stepped down from a little ledge overlooking a gravelly lower shelf that tapered away to level ground. Negotiating the ledge and shelf took special care to avoid kicking a rock or slipping and falling down. At the base of the shelf, I was on soft ground and had only fifty or so paces of grassy expanse between me and the nearest of the three horses. I knelt to put my shoes back on, and for the first time noticed my fingers shaking. Nervously I watched the girl as I fumbled with the laces. Contrary to what she had claimed, she must have been exhausted. Buster, too, must have really been knocked out.

My shoes back on, I turned my attention to the horses. They were staked so that they could not cross over one another's stake ropes and get tangled up, which meant they were spaced some distance apart. The nearest one was a leggy chestnut, Janie's. Next was Buster's rangy black. Farthest of all was my bay—the one I had stolen from Clyde's Creek half-blood "friend."

When I had first left the cave, all three animals had been standing hip-shot, swishing flies. Now they had turned and were looking curiously at me. I circled the first two and attempted to come up easy on the bay. He had other ideas. As I drew close, he snorted and backed away, stretching his stake rope tight. I looked back at the cave and couldn't quite believe that no one there had heard. As I moved closer I started mumbling what I hoped were soothing words. I reached the stake and the rope and leaned down to untie it. The horse stamped his front feet but stayed where he was and did not spook. The moment I had the rope in hand, he must have realized that I was in command, for he stood perfectly still as I moved up to him. I patted him on the neck and said something stupid, like, "Good horsey, nice horsey."

The animal didn't wear a halter; the rope was simply tied around his neck with a knot that would not slip. I eased the bridle headstall over his head and made him take the bit. Then I undid the rope around his neck and tossed it aside. All I needed now was to mount up and be gone.

I led the horse a short distance toward the creek, then glanced back at the cave. There was no sign at all that my absence had been discovered. I grasped a handful of mane with my left hand and prepared to swing aboard the way I had always done with my pa's plow horses back on our Kansas farm. Because of those old plow horses, I guess I had ridden more without a saddle than I ever had with one. I fancied myself pretty good at mounting a barebacked horse.

If that Creek half-blood's bay had been a plow horse, I might have gotten away with it. If he had just crow-hopped around the way he had done when I first mounted him with a saddle on, I might have ridden him right on off and got away. Maybe the Indian never had ridden him bareback. I don't know, but he sure didn't just crow-hop, and I sure didn't ride him. The instant I lit on his back he came apart like fireworks exploding on the Fourth of July. He must have thrown me twelve feet in the air, straight up. I came down so hard and landed so perfectly flat on my back the air just *whooshed* out of me, and for I don't know how long I could only see strange lights surrounded by pure darkness.

My next conscious moment, Janie and her brother were standing over me and Buster was saying, "Boy, am I ever disappointed in you!"

"I don't think you understand your position here very well," Buster was telling me ten minutes later back at the cave. The three of us sat around the fire drinking coffee almost as if nothing had happened. "You see, your membership in this gang may be temporary, but it ain't exactly optional. I don't agree with the idea myself, but Clyde does, which is what counts. And until he decides different, you're just not supposed to go anywhere. Not alone, at least. Not without asking first."

"It isn't something we can blame on him," Janie pointed out. "He only did what you might expect him to do. It was my fault he got the chance. I just didn't realize how tired I was."

"Well, he's just lucky Clyde wasn't here. Or Kansas. Dammit, messenger, you want us to change our minds about shooting you?"

I didn't know how serious he was, but I was determined not to let them think me frightened of them. I only said, "Don't we have anything to eat around here? I'm starving."

There wasn't much food left; only a couple of cans of fruit, some three-day-old biscuits, and coffee. "I always figured train robbers and such planned things better than this," I said, trying a biscuit. "Surely you knew you would need provisions for your getaway."

"It's the nature of our work," Janie said. "We have to travel light."

"Yeah, but *this* light?" We had eaten only very little better the night before.

She gave an indifferent little shrug. "We planned to get what more we needed from Clyde's Indian friend. We didn't expect him to sic that posse on us."

"Or to have Clyde invite a guest," Buster added.

I ignored this. "So what do we do till Clyde gets back? Even with these biscuits, my belly still thinks by throat's been cut. Can't we at least go look for some game? There must be some around—turkeys, squirrels, something we can hunt."

Buster shook his head. "I asked Clyde about that before he left. He said no shooting. Someone might hear. It would be too risky."

I sighed and decided it was essentially hopeless.

Janie was looking at me curiously. "Tell us your name, messenger. What can we call you besides that? Tell us again about how you knew the Daltons back in Coffeyville."

Once more I sighed. The sun was somewhat behind me now, and although I was partially in the shade of a scraggly oak growing to one side of the cave's mouth, I was feeling hot and a little queasy. "My name is T.G.—T. G. Shannon, Jr. I didn't know the Daltons real well. I think they're all older than me—the ones you're talking about, anyway."

"I see," the girl said. "But you do know them when you see them. You knew my brother wasn't Bob Dalton right off. Isn't that right?"

"I knew the minute I saw his face."

"And Buster? When did you know he wasn't Emmett?"

I considered this a moment. "Well, Emmett isn't as skinny as Buster, but I guess I didn't know for certain until I saw him without his mask."

There was a pause, then I said, "Now you tell me something. Your names. Clyde, Buster, Janie. I heard Kansas call Clyde 'Crosby' once. Are those your real names? Clyde, Buster, and Janie Crosby?"

Buster looked suspicious. "Maybe you don't need to know that. Maybe it's just as well you don't know if those are our real names or not."

"But they are, aren't they? I can tell by the way you answer to them. Kansas and Juice are different. Every once in a while one of them almost looks blank when called by those names. But never you or Janie or Clyde. What I don't understand is, why pose as someone you're not? Why put your own bad deeds off on the Daltons? Something *they* might have to answer for when they're caught."

"We pose as someone we're not so no one will know who we really are," he explained patiently. "As for the Daltons, if they've done half of what they're already accused of, they couldn't get off with less than ninety years apiece to save their lives. Besides, no one really thinks those boys can be taken alive. I know I sure don't."

He was right about that, and he could see I knew it. It didn't make what they had done right, but then, robbing trains under any guise wasn't right. I turned to Janie. "And you, what's your opinion of this operation? I know these fellows are your brothers, but why are you in on it? Someone who looks like you — surely some good-looking young fellow has offered to take you away from all this by now. Surely . . ."

A not-so-subtle change came over both of them then. Even a dummy who talks too much could see it. Buster started to say something, but the girl stopped him. She said, "There *was* such a young fellow, T.G. He was my sweetheart from the time I was thirteen years old. I married him the day after I turned seventeen. He had a good job as a bank teller in the town where we lived and we were going to build a house. Three months later he was cut down by a U.S. deputy marshal's bullet in a gunfight during a robbery of the bank where he worked. He was strictly an innocent bystander . . ." Her voice cracked at this point. "He was only twenty-one years old . . ."

I started to say something, to apologize for having intruded, but she waved me off with a flick of the hand. "It's not your fault. You didn't know. My name is Janie Crosby Beaumont; I don't mind if you know that. I am a widow at eighteen, and I would just as soon be running the risks of this business with my brothers as enduring any of the heartache and despair that I've known while doing otherwise."

I didn't feel well at all. I don't know if it was the coffee or the biscuits or simply the heat, but my stomach felt as if it had been punched from the inside. I presently excused myself and went back inside the cave to lie down.

It wasn't very cool in there either, but somehow I fell asleep anyway. When I woke up a while later, the shadows outside had grown long. My stomach felt better but my sore muscles had, if anything, grown even more sore. I groaned as I rolled away from the saddle that was my pillow, and Janie appeared almost as if from nowhere.

"Are you all right?"

"I'm not sure. Do I look all right?"

"Not really."

"Well, if I die, you'll be at least partly responsible," I said sourly.

"I know. And that's beginning to bother me some."

"But not enough to let me go, right?"

"No. Not yet."

I looked around. "Where's Buster?"

"He went down to the river to do some fishing. He thought he might catch a catfish or two for supper. How would that sound to you?"

"How would a fresh pond look to a migrating duck?" I asked. "How would a henhouse look to an egg-sucking dog? How would—?"

"I know. I feel the same way." She smiled.

Somehow I wasn't sure I should get my hopes up. "How does Buster plan to catch these fish? With a club?"

"Oh, no. Buster is quite a fisherman. He always carries some fishing line and a few hooks and sinkers in his saddlebags. He'll find something to make a pole out of, and some worms or grubs or grasshoppers for bait. If anyone can catch something, Buster can."

I pulled my watch from my pocket. "It's almost six o'clock. I've done a little fishing myself; I figure he might be half the night down there."

Janie shrugged. "Then we'll eat late, is all. That will be better than going hungry, won't it?"

"Yes, it will. But look, why wait around? Maybe we can find something else around here. Surely there's a plum thicket or some wild grapes growing along the creek someplace."

She looked at me narrowly. "Are you planning something again? More ideas of escape, maybe?"

"I'm thinking of finding something to eat," I said. "But that doesn't mean I'll make you any promises about anything else. That goes for whatever we do."

She nodded her acceptance of this. "Fair enough. Do you feel up to a hike down to the creek, then?"

"I think so. I think I was mostly tired before. I'm rested now."

I was a bit rocky on my feet, regardless. Probably my poor diet of the last couple of days was responsible. In any event, a few moments of standing and I felt all right to walk.

"You lead," Janie said.

We walked past where the horses were grazing, and I asked if they shouldn't be taken to water. Janie informed me that Buster had done that before he went fishing. We checked their stake ropes to make sure they were well tied and resumed our walk.

Less than a hundred yards separated us from our destination, and we made our way down a faint path that wound through tall grass. Beautiful, towering cottonwoods, with trunks so thick two grown men could hide behind any one of them, lined the creek, while tangled bushes commanded the understory. The creek, just wide enough that it couldn't be jumped, trickled and gurgled with clear water that wasn't cold but was at least cool. We saw no bushes bearing fruit—except a particularly thorny thing that neither of us was familiar with and did not want to chance being poisoned by— and so we were not successful in our mission. We wandered upstream for at least a half a mile, drank from a glassy little pool, and even crossed and recrossed the stream by walking on half-submerged rocks.

Somewhere along the way I forgot that I was a prisoner and that Janie Crosby Beaumont was my keeper. I think maybe she forgot too, at least for a while.

"This is so peaceful," she said once, as I led the way back down the creek. "Wouldn't it be nice if things could be like this always?"

I was busy pushing aside overhanging branches. "It might be all right, assuming one had a few basic necessities of life—such as food, something besides a saddle and a saddle blanket for a bed, a decent roof over one's head—"

"Oh, you are such a sourpuss, T. G. Shannon, Jr.!" she exclaimed. Then she added, "Is that really all they call you—T.G.? What does it stand for? Thomas? Theodore?"

"Terence Gardner Shannon," I said. "I don't like Terence or Gardner much. T.G. is what I've always answered to."

"T.G." She said it over three or four times. "You know, you're kind of nice looking, T.G. Has anybody ever told you that? Have you got a best girl?"

I had a distinct temptation to lie and say yes, but of course that would only have been my pride talking. I wound up compromising with dead honesty by shrugging and saying, "Not really. Not just now."

"Well, that's too bad," Janie said. "Some girl is missing a real bet."

I felt a funny little tingle inside that was beginning to tell me something about my reaction to this girl. I suspect that any impressionable young man who has walked down a lonesome creek-bottom trail just at dusk with a pretty girl knows how it is. But I wasn't about to let myself be overwhelmed by romantic notions. I absolutely was not.

The sun was well down by the time we neared the trail that led back to the cave. We could see the horses still grazing, but there was not much daylight left. Crickets were beginning to chirp. A night bird swooped just over my head. I thought I heard something in the bushes downstream from where we stood.

Janie must have heard it too, for suddenly her hand was on my forearm. "What was that?" she whispered. She stood very close by my side, her right shoulder faintly touching my left. It occurred to me only vaguely then how easily I could have overpowered her. A perfect opportunity. I don't know why I didn't. I guess my mind just wasn't on it then.

The rustling in the bushes grew louder. I motioned Janie back from the trail. We both knew that this was technically still Creek country, although the Osage reservation boundary was near. Either way, an Indian hunter, perhaps? Janie finally remembered her gun, and I guess me as well, for when she drew the weapon she also gave me a strange little look and stepped quickly back. At the same time a lone figure burst out of the bushes along the creek bank and drew up, startled, peering at us.

It was Buster. He stood not twenty feet away, his fishing pole in one hand and what was undoubtedly the finest string of catfish I had ever seen in a long time in the other.

He said, "Now just what the hell are *you* two doing down here?"

CHAPTER 5

WE cleaned the fish — six nice ones — and baked them by spreading them open and laying them on their unskinned backs atop hot coals. Janie had some tin plates and forks inside a canvas sack that she carried on her saddle. It was the same sack that carried her coffeepot and other limited provisions. When the fish were cooked, we forked them onto plates and picked the flesh from between the bones from the inside. They tasted a little of Arkansas River mud, but far be it from me to complain, was the way I looked at it.

"This works better on bass or crappie," Buster said. "But since we don't have anything to fry them in, this is at least a way to do it."

I was so hungry I didn't care. I ate two whole fish and half of one Janie couldn't finish. My stomach hurt, I was so full, but it was the best hurt I had known in a long time.

"Doesn't look like Clyde's coming back tonight," I said a little later as we sat around the fire. Buster was busy rolling a cigarette; Janie and I were still sipping from mugs of steaming hot coffee.

"Maybe, maybe not," Buster said. "Night's young yet. They could come at any time."

"As much as I like catfish," I said, "some bacon and fresh bread would sure taste good in the morning."

Buster gave me a quizzical stare. "You sure do worry a lot about your stomach. I guess you haven't missed many meals in your lifetime."

"No, I suppose I haven't," I admitted. "But you have, of course."

"Don't let him fool you, T.G.," Janie warned. "We aren't, and never were, poor white trash who never had a break in life. My brothers aren't outlaws because they were raised dirt poor and think the world owes them a living."

"Then why are they outlaws?" I asked.

Janie transferred her gaze to Buster, as if that was a question *somebody* should be able to answer.

Buster shrugged it off. "You'd have to *be* an outlaw to understand."

"Yeah? Well, try me. Is it the excitement? Or is it only the money?"

Buster looked at me as if I was something he'd die to get rid of. "You sound like some poor dope asking a whore why she's in the business she's in." And then he grinned mischievously. "Tell me, messenger, have you ever asked a whore that? Have you ever—?"

"Buster!" It was Janie, blushing. "You have no right to ask that!"

"He's asking me stuff," Buster insisted self-righteously. "What's the matter, little sister? You think this boy never did anything like that? You taking a liking to him, are you?"

"Buster! Stop it!"

Her brother had the air of a man who knew he had just turned the tables on someone. "You two was looking awful friendly down by the creek a while ago. I sure did notice that."

Janie gave her brother an absolutely withering look. "You are a real dunce, Buster! An absolute dunce!" Then she tossed what was left of her coffee into the fire and flung her cup off to one side. The fire spit angrily and the cup banged against a rock and went rolling across the ground. Janie whirled and stormed off into the darkness, slipping on the lip of the ledge as she went but not falling.

Buster watched her disappear. "My, my. I think I hit a nerve."

"Could be," I said, still a little shocked.

Neither of us said anything else for almost a minute. I suppose we both thought Janie might come right back. She didn't and we couldn't even hear her out there.

"That's a real snit my sister's in," Buster finally said. When I didn't reply, he seemed compelled to add, "It's kind of unusual of her."

I only nodded, as if I had no doubt that what he said was true.

He went on, "She's still mourning that Billy Beaumont, I reckon. She acts like it ain't proper to even hint that she might be interested in somebody else."

I nodded again, thoughtfully, silently.

"I don't know why I said what I did. Fact is, I didn't see a damn thing down at that creek. Ain't that hell? Not a single damn thing."

I had slept so much during the day I wasn't tired, and neither was Buster. Janie, I think, was pretty worn out. She came back after being gone about thirty minutes, and when she did it was almost as if nothing had happened.

She gathered up her bedroll and tossed it off to one side, just outside the cave. "I'm going to turn in. You two can stay up and talk however long you like."

Buster said, "Are we gonna tie him up this time?"

Janie's eyes met mine with what I felt was true sympathy. "I'm sorry, T.G. You haven't left us much choice."

I shrugged. "I'm really not sleepy anyway. Maybe you could just lean my saddle against the side of the cave over there and tie my hands in front of me. That way I can at least sit up, have something to lean on, and be halfway comfortable at the same time."

Buster looked at me as if I was stupid; Janie seemed amused. "Behind you, T.G. We'll have to tie your hands behind you. You know that."

I sighed. "Yeah, I know. But I think I'd even promise not to try to get away if you'd at least tie the ropes loose enough they don't cut the circulation off. You probably don't know how miserable a feeling that is."

"Would your promise mean anything this time?"

"If I actually say 'I promise,' it would. Before, you worked something out of me I really didn't mean."

An hour later I sat leaning against my saddle, trussed up about the way I had requested. Janie had already gone to her bedroll and seemed fast asleep. Buster had dragged his saddle over to within ten feet of me and was stretched out, using the saddle as a headrest. He had his head propped so he could look directly at me.

"I ain't quite so trusting as my sister," he explained. "I think I'll just watch you from here, maybe all night. And just because we haven't killed you yet, don't get the idea I won't if I have to."

Ten minutes later he caught himself about to doze off. He must have realized he wasn't going to make it through the night. "Well, anyway," he said, shifting his position to something more comfortable. "Wouldn't do you no good to get away anyhow. The Osage or Creek police would probably just catch you and shoot you for a horse thief. Which is what that bay horse out there makes you, you know — a horse thief running with an outlaw gang."

The worst thing about all of that business was, he made me think how some of it just might be true. That and my promise to Janie, I guess, was one reason I didn't try to squirm my way over to him after he was asleep and steal his gun. The way they'd tied me, I believe I could have very easily.

Janie put the last of our coffee on to boil at sunup. Then she saw that I was awake and watching her, and came over and untied me. While she was doing this, Buster sat up and looked around as if he hadn't the least idea where he was.

"Well," I said brightly, "I see we are all still here."

Buster blinked, then glared at me. "Don't be smart, messenger." Then he added, "Dammit, I sure was hoping Clyde and them would come in during the night."

"I take it you slept well," Janie remarked, smiling.

Buster didn't react to this, except to glance somewhat strangely at me. I suppose it was a warning that I had better not say anything. He said to Janie, "I don't reckon there's anything left to eat."

"One three-day-old biscuit and two-thirds of a can of pears apiece," she told him.

"Gosh, I wish I could do arithmetic like that," he moaned sarcastically. After a moment he looked off in the direction of the river. "I think I'll go fishing again after breakfast. You two wanta come along?"

"Well, maybe it would at least break the monotony," Janie speculated. "What do you think, T.G.?"

"Sure," I said. "Anything to break the monotony."

"Good," Buster said. "Only this time we'll take the horses. I don't wanta get put on foot in case someone stumbles onto this place while we're gone."

An hour later we found ourselves on a shady, grassy bank of the Arkansas, near where our small creek entered it, digging worms, cutting poles, tying on lines and hooks and sinkers, and trying to follow Buster's instructions regarding where and how to toss our baits. Giant trees and thick underbrush hid us from virtually all view. Our horses were tied twenty yards away, in the brush, and they too were well concealed.

Buster said, "If Clyde and the boys show up during the day, we should be able to see them cross the river from here."

"Will they do that?" I asked. "Cross in broad daylight?"

Buster's forehead knitted in a frown. "I dunno. If they're not being chased, they might. Dammit, I sure do wish they would've showed up last night."

Janie cast him a suspicious glance. "You do know how to get to the Triangle camp from here, don't you, Buster?"

Her brother didn't look as if he wanted to answer this. He mumbled something unintelligible.

"You *don't* know?"

"I can get there," he maintained with some finality.

The conversation sort of died at that point, and I found myself peering at my fishing line, which had been pulled straight by the current but was barely visible from my angle against the dark water. The day was still young, the morning shadows long — not a bad time for the fish to be biting. After a moment, I thought I detected a light tug against my line. When it happened again, I leaned intently forward and my fingers tightened around by fishing pole.

"He's getting a bite," Buster said. "Look at him."

With the fourth tug, I yanked back as if I was setting the hook on a whale. The pole was stout and did not bend much; whatever was on the other end was equally unyielding.

"Hey!" Buster exclaimed. "He's got a big one!"

I stood up, not entirely sure what to do. Of course there was no reel with which to bring in my catch; only me and the pole and the line. Buster rushed forward to help me, grabbing the line and hauling away at it, hand over hand.

"Back up!" he ordered. "Back up!"

I did as I was told, but slipped on some wet grass and lost my footing. I hit the ground hard, temporarily losing my grip on the fishing pole. Janie, I guess seeing this, came quickly to try to help out. She grabbed for the pole, and in the process lost her balance too. She fell just as I was struggling to get back up, sprawling across me. The two of us went down in a heap and the pole went flying.

Buster, left attempting to haul in line all alone, must have sensed something wrong behind him. "Hey! What the hell!"

Janie lay across my chest, our faces within inches of one another, the very special softness of her breast contrasting wildly with the boniness of mine. I was so giddily distracted I forgot all about the fishing pole, the fish, and Buster. My eyes were locked on Janie's, my efforts to rise completely stilled.

"Oh, T.G.!" she finally murmured. "Did I hurt you? Can't you breath?"

I guess I was sort of gasping, but not for the reason she thought. She lifted herself away from me, but only to crouch over me on her knees. For the longest moment, her eyes did not leave mine.

"What the hell are you two doing?" It was Buster. He had turned around and was looking at us in the strangest way. In one hand he held a short section of fishing line and dangling from this was a huge, lumpy-fat catfish, weighing surely no less than four pounds.

"We fell," Janie explained simply. "I think T.G. got the wind knocked out of him."

Buster looked from his sister to me to the fishing pole, now lying uselessly off to one side. Holding the catfish up high, he shook both his fist and the fish at us. "Well, while you were doing that, T.G. also caught himself a fish. Bigger than any two of the ones I caught last night."

I couldn't tell if he was angry with me for tumbling around on the riverbank with his sister or if he was simply jealous of my fish — which of course I never could have landed without him.

I was about to make the diplomatic gesture of pointing this out to him when something across the river suddenly caught my eye. A horse and rider had appeared on a sunny patch of bank there, maybe a hundred yards upstream from us. It seemed clear that the rider had intentions of fording. Buster saw me looking and turned to follow my gaze. The rider spurred his horse into the river just as Buster turned.

"Who do you suppose he is?" I asked, sitting up.

Janie, getting to her feet beside me, said, "That horse looks an awful lot like Kansas's bay."

Buster squinted hard. "If it is, why is he alone?"

Nobody had an answer to that. Nonetheless, the horse definitely was a bay, and the rider was dressed in dark clothing much the same as Kansas had worn when we last saw him. Still, we could not be sure until they drew closer. I too was on my feet by the time Janie cried out, "Oh, it *is* Kansas! I'm sure of it!" She then proceeded to wave and call to him, and one could actually see a smile on his face as he waved back.

A minute later the horse lurched onto the bank, dripping, and Kansas dismounted in front of us. "Well, what an easy life this looks to be!" he said. "Some bunch of train robbers you all must be!"

"Some of us aren't train robbers at all," I pointed out from off to one side.

Kansas turned my way. "Why, hello, messenger. Say, I have something here you might be interested in."

As he turned to his horse and began a search through his saddle-bags, Buster asked, "Where's Clyde? Where's Juice?"

"They won't be coming for a day or two, and then it'll only be to meet us at the Triangle camp. I'm supposed to make sure you get there okay." He finally produced a couple of wadded-up newspapers from inside one of the saddlebags and handed them to me. "We made the papers, messenger. And so did you. Clyde thought you'd be interested."

I sat down to read while the others regarded me curiously. I don't remember now the name of either newspaper, but each had a headline and a story in it about the robbery of my Katy train. They must have been among the first reports out, for they weren't terribly accurate. One account showed no hesitancy at all in attributing the robbery to the Daltons; the other reflected less certainty about who the outlaws were. Both mentioned me by name as the express messenger who had been taken by the robbers, and to my horror, one even speculated that I had been in on the escapade from the start, that I was an inside man for the gang — *whoever* they were — and that the kidnapping was strictly a staged event.

CHAPTER 6

KANSAS had with him a burlap sack filled with food and supplies, so we went on back up to the cave to see what we could put together to eat. While Buster and I were skinning and filleting the catfish, Janie was digging a brand-new skillet, flour, salt, coffee, and some other items out of the sack. Kansas brought a coffeepot full of water up from the creek, gave Janie just enough to mix up some bread dough, and then put the rest on a freshly built fire to boil for coffee. He also has something for me: the spanking-new makings of a bedroll—two balnkets and a light tarp—that he had carried rolled and tied on the back of his saddle atop his own bedroll.

"Here," he said, tossing them to me. "Clyde said you oughta have this. Hope you appreciate it."

"Don't worry about that," I said as I gladly tied the bedroll onto the back of my own saddle.

A while later, we had pan bread, fried catfish fillets, and peach preserves. I don't think I ever ate much better.

"The doc wanted to amputate Juice's foot," Kansas told us, "but the little knothead wouldn't hear of it."

"So what are they gonna do—him and Clyde?" Buster wanted to know. "Where are they now?"

"They're laying low over at Ingalls, which is a hard day's ride west of here—and an even harder night's back, let me tell you. The doc there did what he could for Juice's foot and told him to hang around till he could be sure it wasn't gonna get infected. I think he was hoping he could still convince the damn fool it should come off, but he don't know Juice. I figure when it's all said and done, they could even beat us to the camp."

"Aren't they afraid they'll get caught?" I asked, looking over at

Kansas's horse. I realized for the first time that although the animal was a bay, it was not the same horse he had ridden out on something over twenty-four hours earlier. It stood to reason: One horse could never have survived the round trip between Ingalls and where we were in so short a time. This animal had been acquired somewhere along the way, and very possibly was stolen. "What about the law? Are there no posses out looking for this gang?"

Kansas didn't look concerned. "They don't know who they're looking for. Mostly everybody's still hunting the Daltons. Like it says in those newspapers, at least some folks are still thinking that job of ours was one of theirs. That's why Clyde says you stay with us. He doesn't want you letting the cat out of the bag."

I stared at him. "Look, if I'm such a threat to you, why haven't you just killed me? That would be the simplest way, you know."

Kansas gave me a sober look. "We've talked about it, messenger, you better believe we have. But Clyde says no killing unless we have to; that's the rule of the gang—no one wants to hang if he don't have to. We're to shoot you only if you try to get away."

"This gang ain't gonna be forever," Buster offered. "We're in it for a big stake. Soon as that happens, why, we'll go our own separate ways, maybe leave the country for good. Could be Clyde'll let you go then."

I didn't feel much comforted by this; I felt even less so when Kansas added with a chuckle, "Besides, messenger, they got you tagged as one of us. Didn't you read that story? They think you were in cahoots with the train robbers!"

"And the longer I stay with you," I said, not laughing, "the harder it's going to be for me to clear myself of that. Don't you see what's going to happen to me when you finally do turn me loose? I'll be an outlaw too!"

"Then you're just as well off with us," he argued. "Hell, we know how to dodge the law; you don't. Talk to Clyde; maybe he'll even cut you in. Then you'll be rich like us and won't have to ride them noisy, sooty old trains anymore."

"I don't want to be an outlaw," I maintained stubbornly. "I liked riding trains just fine."

"Then you shouldn't have stole that half-blood's horse. That's a crime, messenger. An absolute crime."

I was so tired of hearing that from them I could have yelled. "I am not a horse thief! You people made me ride off on that Indian's horse. *You* are the horse thieves, not me!"

"Try telling that to the Indian," Kansas drawled. "Try telling it to the posse that drags you in to face old Hangin' Judge Parker over at the Fort Smith, Arkansas federal court when you're caught and charged with aiding and abetting a train robbery in Indian Territory. Why, you'll stutter and stammer like there was cotton in your mouth and mother's milk going to clabber in your veins. That's what you'll do."

"Oh, leave him alone, Kansas," Janie finally put in tiredly. "T.G., you should know by now that he's only trying to get your goat, just the way he always does poor Juice. The only thing he's right about is that we are not a bunch of cold-blooded killers. You should talk to Clyde. When we get to the Triangle camp, then we'll see."

I sighed. It hardly seemed any use. Unless and until I could find a way to escape, I was strictly stuck with the situation.

And so I saddled up just like they did an hour later, ready to begin the ride to their hideout between the Cimarron and the Arkansas. I saddled that fool bay horse and plainly dared him to pitch with me when I mounted. He just stood there and didn't even twitch.

I looked back at the cave as we rode away and wondered what my memories of it would someday be. I have read much speculation since then about a similar cave hideout the Daltons themselves were supposed to have used that very summer of 1892. It was said to be located "somewhere west of Tulsa." I never could learn for sure if the Daltons really did use such a hideout. I do know that there appears to be some doubt. Because of this, I've often wondered if someone didn't stumble onto some sign of our presence at the cave after we had left and maybe judge that an outlaw gang had holed up there. It would have been like them, in those days, to just naturally assume we had been the Daltons.

We made camp late that afternoon beneath blackjack oak and walnut trees, in a hilly country that Kansas said was definitely Osage territory, and beside a small stream with water so clear that we decided it must surely be springfed. We had not seen a single sign of another human being all day, and because of this, Kansas was not hesitant to do a little hunting. He went off by himself while we were making camp, fired maybe fifteen shots over a period of forty-five minutes, and came back with eight plump squirrels, each shot through the head. Buster remarked for my benefit that Kansas was a crack shot; I hardly needed to be told.

Well past dark, we cooked the squirrels over an open fire, and I think as we ate them I enjoyed each bite more than the one before. Kansas sat across from me, and about halfway through the meal I noticed him regarding me thoughtfully.

"You know, messenger, we're gonna have to get you a hat somewhere. Your face is beginning to look like a boiled beet."

I hadn't seen my face lately, but did not doubt that he was right. My lips were badly chapped, too. As an express messenger I had worn a cap, but that had been left on the train during the robbery. I really did need a hat.

"Maybe we could ride mostly in the early morning and late afternoon," Janie suggested. "We could hole up during the heat of the day somewhere. I think Clyde left an extra hat he might use at the Triangle camp, but there certainly isn't any way he can get one between here and there."

"That's true," Kansas said, treating it seriously. "What size do you wear, messenger?"

"To be honest, I really don't know. Most of my hats have been hand-me-downs. Not many of them ever fit."

"I see," he said. "Well, I figure we can make the Triangle camp by late tomorrow if we put in a day; by noon the next day if we dawdle. It's up to the three of you. Don't much matter to me."

"When will we cross the Arkansas again?" Buster wanted to know.

Kansas thought about it. "If we get a good start, I'd say by midmorning. We could camp for the main part of the day on the opposite bank. We could fish, swim, sleep—whatever anybody wants to do."

Buster seemed to like this idea, but Janie had at least one reservation. "I will *not* watch you men swim again!"

Kansas looked hurt. "Why not, pray tell?"

"You *know* why not," she shot back. "You always go naked. I watched once, accidentally—when nobody warned me. Never again!"

"All right," Kansas said, shrugging. "You swim and we'll watch. I don't care."

She didn't even bother to reply to this. Instead, she looked away, beyond the firelight in the direction of the little clear-watered stream that ran nearby. "You know, I think I would like to bathe. It's been days now, and I just hate being sweaty and dirty . . ."

"It's dark out there, Janie," Buster reminded her. "I don't think you oughta be wandering around alone."

"That never bothered you before," she retorted, rising.

"It's also a very small stream. You'll be lucky to even get wet."

"I saw a little pool earlier," she said, gathering up our plates, on which we'd had biscuits and preserves to go with the squirrel. "It's not far. You fellows can clean up the dishes while I'm gone."

"That's what I was afraid of," Buster moaned.

Janie sat the supper utensils down beside him and said dryly, "Just remember, I can see the lot of you from there. I'll know if any of you leave the fire. Don't you dare come my way!"

I was wondering how we were going to take care of the dishwashing without going down to the creek and chancing an encounter with Janie at her bath, when Buster looked at me and I realized it wasn't going to be a matter of "we" at all. It was *me* about to win an uncontested election.

I shrugged. "What do I do — scour them with dirt from around the fire?"

"Hell, no!" he said. "The stuff around here is damn near pure clay and won't scour worth a damn. You need at least some sand for that. No matter what Janie says, you'll have to go to the creek." He had one of those devilish grins on his face that I didn't like at all.

I looked at Kansas, then back at Buster. "You're setting me up. I won't do it. Not until she gets back."

His grin faded and his eyes flashed challengingly. "Them plates and things have to be cleaned *before* she gets back, messenger. Otherwise, she'll think we left them for her. Now, you wouldn't wanta do my sister that way, would you?"

"I'll go when she gets back," I said stubbornly, "but not now."

Buster's eyes widened in mock surprise and indignation. He glanced at Kansas. "What'd I tell you about this fellow not understanding his place around here? Now look, messenger, what we're talking about here is a job that's got to be done. It ain't much of a job and don't require much talent, but it's the kind of thing a new member of the gang gets to do."

I must not have looked very receptive to any of this, because

Kansas decided to mediate. "Oh, come on, boy. There'll be no harm done. Janie went downstream, and you can go up. It's dark and you won't see a thing. And look here, if you'll do it, why, I think we might even let you sleep tonight without tying you up. What would you say to that?"

"I'd say I don't believe you. You'd never do that."

Kansas tried to look hurt. "*What?* You think I'd lie to you? Golly. Well, let me put it this way. Only a fool would try to escape from here, and I don't think you're that fool. Hell, this is Osage country, boy. Much of it's a wilderness. You could be lost for days. And look here, these Indian tribes have their own police, and the Osages are some of the best. What's more, they think every lone white man wandering around in their country is a horse thief. They might shoot first and ask whose bay horse that is later. You see what I mean?"

I was becoming accustomed to this kind of talk, and I guess they had me about half convinced. More to the point, however, I was trying desperately to remember what it was like to sleep without being tied up like a stack of letters about to be tossed onto a mail car. Surely it wouldn't be too hard to convince Janie that I had only been going to the creek to wash those dishes.

I met Kansas's gaze. "You really won't tie me up? You mean it?"

"I've never been so truthful. Absolutely never."

Whether I should have known better or not becomes a moot question now. I'm sure I did know better. They were entirely too mischievous in their determination to send me out there for me to trust them fully. But I wanted very badly to believe the part about them not tying me up.

Finally I sighed and started gathering up the utensils that needed washing. "I just hope I can see what I'm doing out there," I said. "I don't want to lose half this stuff in the dark."

"Here, take Janie's provisions sack and this old towel she uses," Kansas said. "Put the plates and stuff in there after you wash 'em."

That sounded reasonable, and moments later I stumbled off into the night with plates, coffee cups, and silverware stacked so that I could carry both them and Janie's sack at the same time. I had the towel draped over my shoulder.

Once beyond the firelight, I stopped to let my eyes adjust to the darkness. I thought I could hear chuckling behind me, but I decided to pay it no mind. Directly ahead of me, I could hear the calming trickle of the little stream. It could hardly have been thirty paces away. The moon the past few nights had been waning from full, and thus rose later each night. I figured it would be fifteen minutes or so yet before it made an appearance. Still, there were all those thousands of stars in a perfectly clear sky, and as my eyes adjusted I began to make a few things out.

I went the way Kansas and Buster had said to go, feeling my way carefully through weeds and tall grass, past a thick clump of bushes, to a giant walnut that grew on the creek bank. I waited a moment to see if my eyes would adjust further, then dropped Janie's sack lightly to the ground and knelt at the water's edge. I set the dishes and things beside me with the intention of washing each item, wiping it dry, and placing it in the sack before going on to the next one.

I was just reaching for the first coffee cup when I heard something not far downstream from me splash lightly in the water. I tried to see what had caused the noise, but could not make out a thing. I could speculate, though, and my guess was that it was no animal over there.

This was confirmed quickly enough by a loudly whispered, "T.G., is that you?"

For a moment I froze. "Yeah," I finally mumbled. "Yeah, it's me." Kansas had said that she would be downstream and I would be upstream. Just naturally, I had assumed some *distance* down and up from one another. Judging from her whisper and the splashing sounds I had heard, I decided we couldn't have been over thirty feet apart.

"I saw you leaving the fire. Can . . . you see me?"

I could only hope the truth would sound convincing. "No. It's too dark. I almost can't see my own hands."

"That had better be true," she warned.

"Why? Haven't you got your clothes on?"

"Ssssh! Don't talk so loud! Those two hyenas back in camp will hear you!" There was a pause. "Don't you dare look over here, T.G. Don't you dare!"

I was fumbling with the third of four coffee cups, reaching for Janie's make-do dish towel. "I'm not looking. I'm washing the dishes. Are you at least getting dressed?"

A distinct moment of hesitation was followed by, "I—I'm trying. I'm about . . . half dressed, I guess you could say."

"Half dressed? What do you mean by that? Which half?"

"The bottom half," she said. "I can't find my shirt anywhere. I laid it right here on the bank with my pants, but now I can't find it. I — I've looked everywhere; I've *felt* everywhere. I simply cannot find it, and I haven't a stitch to wear underneath it or instead of it."

I wondered if failure to control one's imagination was sinful. I dropped the fourth cup in the creek, and only a lucky swipe with my left hand fished it back out before it floated away.

"It must be there someplace," I said. "Unless you accidentally kicked it into the creek. You didn't do that, did you?"

"Oh God, I hope not! Dammit, T.G., why did you have to suggest that?"

"I don't know. Look around. It's gotta be somewhere."

"I *have* looked around. I can't find it."

"Do you want me to come and help you?"

"Don't be funny."

I finished the forks and started on the plates. "Your brother and Kansas knew you'd see me leave the fire," I told her. "They figured it would be funny if you thought I was down here trying to peep on you."

"If you knew all that," she asked, a little testily, "how did they talk you into it?"

"They told me these dishes ought to be washed before you got back. I didn't exactly buy that, but then Kansas promised if I'd do it, they wouldn't tie me up for the night. I figured it was worth the risk, just to see if they would keep their word."

"Oh heavens, T.G.! You would believe something like that!"

"I didn't say I believed it. I just took a chance on it, is all. And besides, I'm getting the dishes washed and I can't see a thing over there where you are, and what the devil am I hurting?"

Somehow it seemed as if my eyes must have continued adjusting to the dark, for things suddenly seemed to have grown much lighter. I noticed it first in the amount of reflection on the creek surface, then in the form of shadows being thrown to my right by the big walnut tree. I looked back over my shoulder. A half-risen moon gleamed at me between the trees. It was a beautiful moon. Very large, creamy gold. A pitch-dark night was suddenly beginning to look like day.

I turned back to the next-to-last plate. Almost afraid to look in

Janie's direction, I scrubbed the plate with creek sand and rinsed it off before wiping it dry. I put it in the sack and felt for the last plate.

"Have you found the shirt yet?" I called softly to Janie.

"No, dammit, no," she said. She sounded very exasperated, yet her light cursing hardly seemed unladylike. In those days, not many real ladies could get away with that. Janie always could. It never diminished her one bit in my mind, and I don't think it should have in anyone else's, either.

I shoved the last plate inside the sack, and without thinking about it glanced downstream and across the creek. I didn't expect to see her, so it was something of a shock when I did. A low-growing group of bushes on my side of the creek threw moon shadows that just failed to reach her. She was upright, on her knees, looking around, and the skin of her upper body gleamed white in the soft moonlight. She was facing me and was even closer than I had previously thought. I guess she didn't see me; she was looking down.

I hadn't seen much female nudity in my life, and my mouth was dry and my heart thumping so crazily I thought it would never beat normally again as I somehow forced myself to look away.

Suddenly Janie exclaimed, "Oh, T.G.! I've found it! I've found my shirt! I was looking in the wrong place all the time! It was to my left and not my right! Oh, what a relief!"

I didn't look at her. With the provisions sack already in hand, I rose. "That's good, Janie. I'm through now and I'm going back to camp. See you there, okay?"

"Sure," she said distractedly. "Sure, T.G. I'll be right there. You know, if it hadn't been for that moon coming up I never would have . . ."

Her words trailed off. Possibly it was because the thought had finally occurred to her that I might have got a look at her there in the moonlight. I had no way of knowing, and was not about to ask. I went all the way back to camp and did not once look back.

CHAPTER 7

I have to give it to Kansas and Buster. They were supremely disappointed when, as if by unspoken agreement, neither Janie nor I said a word about anything happening out there in the darkness. They really had expected Janie to be boiling mad, and me (whether I had seen anything or not) to get the chastising of my life for having gone to the creek while she was still there. Instead, Janie simply thanked me for having done the dishes and went straight to her bedroll. I dragged my gear over to a spot near Kansas and Buster and off-handedly inquired if the two erstwhile mischief-makers were going to keep their part of the bargain and not tie me up. Surprisingly, they never argued. I hadn't given them credit for being good sports at all, and thus they each proved something to me that night.

"Just remember, though," Kansas warned. "I may not sleep light, but I sleep with my hand on my gun. And even if you was to get away, we'd track you and catch you the next day for sure — assuming the Indian police didn't get you first, that is."

Even at its best, sleeping on the ground had never been very comfortable for me. But that night, when they let me try it untied and inside my new bedroll, I not only lacked the intention of trying to get away but had visions of pleasant slumber like even those with feather beds never know. Despite this, I had a surprising amount of trouble falling asleep.

Partly, I think, my conscience was bothering me — for having watched Janie down by the creek, for just being there knowing I might see her like that, for even the few unbelievably exciting moments I took to turn away. But mostly it was something else. Something more even than that vivid picture I had of her half-nude form as she knelt there on the bank and looked for her shirt. It was something I would have chosen not to have happen, because it only further complicated my already uncertain situation with the outlaw gang. But what might have been apparent sooner, had I been willing to admit it, was now nigh-on undeniable. I had fallen in love with Janie Crosby Beaumont, and it was to prove an affliction for which even time would prove no remedy.

We reached the Arkansas at midmorning the next day, just as Kansas had predicted we would, but we were two hours more finding a decent place to cross it. When the fording was finally accomplished, we were some distance upriver from where we had first encountered the stream, and Kansas admitted unhappily that he was not familiar with the surroundings on the other side.

"There's a big bend in the river upstream," Buster pointed out. "That should be a good landmark."

"It would be if I'd ever seen it before," Kansas lamented. "It don't mean a thing to me as it is."

"I thought Clyde said you knew the way, Buster," Janie said. "Now we find out neither you nor Kansas seems to know anything."

"Clyde meant we could *find* the way," Buster retorted. "Don't worry, we're not lost."

Kansas looked less confident, but did not say anything. Janie shook her head in wonderment. "Well, in the meantime, why don't we find a place to put up for the day. Look at poor T.G. — he's about to bake in this sun."

We went back downstream about two miles and once again located ourselves on a shady bank of the Arkansas River, only this time for the rest of the day. Buster was especially amenable to this because it gave him a chance to resume his fishing. As if to prove this, he quickly went to work cutting willow poles and tying on line, while I dug for worms with a sharpened stick and Janie set about fixing up something to eat for lunch. Kansas, who wasn't interested in fishing, took care of the horses, then traipsed on downstream to see if he could locate a good spot to swim. When he had gone, Buster and I began fishing, and Janie lay down in the shade, a good nap apparently in mind.

I was sitting there, lost in thought, when Buster suddenly got a bite. Quick as a cat, he reached for his fishing pole, raised it, then held it poised over the water, watching for a second tug on the line. In a moment it came, and Buster yanked hard on the line.

His anticipation was replaced almost instantly by disappointment. "Damn it, I missed him!" He started hauling in line to check his bait.

Less than a minute later, I got a bite. Only seconds after that I had something hooked and was hauling it ashore. Buster watched curiously as I landed a nice foot-long catfish and went to work removing the hook and putting my catch on a makeshift stringer that Buster had fashioned from a piece of small-diameter rope. I tied the stringer to a bush and tossed the fish back in the water.

"I guess they're starting to bite now," I remarked casually as I threaded a new crawler onto my hook. "Maybe we'll catch a real mess before it's over."

"Yeah, maybe we will," Buster said somewhat ill-humoredly as he tossed his own line back into the water.

Five minutes later I had another fish about the same size as the first, and Buster's stare was now more envious than curious. He hadn't even had another bite.

"Don't worry," I told him. "You'll probably catch the next two while I just sit and watch."

He didn't say anything at all to this.

I tossed a freshly baited hook back out and watched the line pull straight as it sank with the current.

"I wish I had some chicken livers," Buster mumbled. "Now there's a real catfish bait. That or a good mix of blood bait. You're doing all right with those worms, messenger, but you ain't never seen no action compared to what I could do with a real bait."

I nodded agreeably and turned just in time to see my line jerk and my pole bob so hard it almost came out of my hands. I yanked back and set the hook into what I was sure was my biggest catch yet. Moments later I had a nice fifteen incher flopping at my feet, and Buster actually groaned from nearby.

I had to dig the hook out of this baby with my pocket knife, and as I slipped the stringer through its mouth and out one gill, Buster came over and said, "Let me see how you're baiting that hook. You must be gobbing worms on like we had ten pounds of 'em."

I had a fruit tin full of moist earth and worms, and I pulled a fat crawler out and threaded it onto my hook. The thing squirmed wildly as I got ready to toss back out.

"Humph," was all Buster said. He went back to his own idle pole and started reeling in the line by winding it around one hand. I watched him strip a limp worm from his hook and start fishing around in his own fruit tin for a fresh one.

"Hook him so he wriggles real good," I suggested helpfully.

"I know how to do it," he grumped. "You just watch. This time it's my turn."

I was beginning to hope it was. I was having fun at this, but I didn't want to spoil it by putting Buster into a pout over it. I was certainly willing to hope for a little parity between us, even if it meant me not catching anything else all day.

I guess catfish don't know about parity, however, for moments later I was hauling in line again. It didn't help much that this was my smallest fish yet; Buster eyed the thing as if I had just stolen his best girl.

"Maybe if we switched places," I offered. "You come over here and toss out where I've been catching them. I'll try your spot for a while."

Grudgingly, he agreed. He brought in his line and we switched spots. A minute or so later he had tossed his bait where I had been placing mine, and I tossed mine where he had been placing his. While this was going on, Kansas came strolling back into view from downriver and Janie gave up on getting much of a nap.

Kansas, his hair still wet from his swim, came up and plopped down beside Buster. Janie came over to stand beside me.

"How's it going, fellows?" Kansas wanted to know. "Is Buster catching all the fish?"

I deferred with a shrug to Buster, and Buster said something that did not resemble any real words. Kansas reached down to inspect my stringer of fish—which I had left at my old spot—and whistled low as he lifted them out of the water. I looked up at Janie and was rewarded with a somewhat knowing smile, which indicated to me that she was aware of all that had been going on.

I almost dreaded watching my own line, and so was concentrating hopefully on Buster's when Janie said, "You're getting a bite, T.G. Better be ready."

I fiddled around at it, almost hoping I would miss him when I tried to set the hook. Even deliberate inexpertise didn't help; the fish hooked itself and bent my pole almost to the breaking point before I could get a hand on the line.

This fish was definitely larger than the others, and it took both Janie and me to get it on the bank.

"Well, well," Kansas said, coming over to me. "That oughta just about round out supper."

Buster wouldn't even look at the fish.

I said, "I think I'll quit with this one. I've never had such a run of luck. Janie, you or Kansas want to fish in my place?"

Kansas said, "Sure, let me have that pole," and came to take my place on the bank. I went over to put my fifth and largest fish on the stringer and had just stepped past a doleful Buster when suddenly that individual gave out a whoop and sat back on his line.

"Hey, look!" I said. "Buster's got one!"

Buster scrambled to his feet as his pole bent in a pronounced arc. "Get back!" he yelled. "This is a big one . . . By God, it's gonna be the biggest one yet!"

Everyone gave him room. Whatever he had hooked was so strong he couldn't even risk working his way up the pole with one hand to grab the line. He backed up a step or two, and all that happened was the pole bent dangerously more. I wasn't sure, but I thought I even heard the tiniest cracking sound.

"Better give to him a little, Buster," I warned. "I think he really is a big one."

Buster didn't say a word; his concentration was solely on his task. When the fish finally began to let up a bit, Buster said, "There, by damn, he's tiring. I've got him now—"

And then it happened. The fish gave a renewed surge and something (we all knew instantly what) went *snap!* Buster, with maybe the weirdest look I ever saw on any human's face, suddenly went plummeting backward and landed hard on the seat of his pants. Janie, Kansas, and I could only look on in shock as he sat there holding approximately one half of his fishing pole and staring at it as if someone has just handed him a rattlesnake.

He looked so ludicrous and miserable sitting there that not even Kansas dared say anything. Even fifteen minutes later, as Kansas and I skinned my five fish a dozen or so yards down the bank from him, not a word had been spoken to or by Buster. He just sat there, glaring at the spot in the river where he had last seen the other end of his fishing pole. He wouldn't even look at the fish we were cleaning; he wouldn't watch later as they were being cooked. We almost couldn't get him to eat any of them when it came time to do that.

"It was probably just a big old carp," Kansas confided to me with a wink. "He wouldn't have been happy with one of those if he'd landed it."

All Buster would ever say about it was, "The first thing I'm gonna buy when I get the chance is some good fishing equipment. A good stout rod with a crank reel, by God—the first place I go where they got one . . ."

He said this to Janie and Kansas. He wouldn't even talk to me until halfway through the following day.

CHAPTER 8

WE broke camp an hour and a half past sunup and struck off in a southerly direction in hopes of locating the outlaws' camp before noon. The countryside was largely wooded, especially the bottoms, but there were also open areas of fine grass dotted with grazing cattle. Kansas told me the cattle belonged to the Bar X Bar ranch, which was operated by a couple of fellows named Hewins and Bennett. Actually, the land was of Cherokee ownership, but because of its isolated location, sandwiched between the two rivers and the reservations of other tribes, it had remained a virtual wilderness and was essentially unsettled even by Indians. For this reason, outlaws gravitated to it, coming and going at will and usually without much bother from the law. They were not much bothered by the Bar X Bar people or the few other full-time inhabitants, either. This was true as long as they honored the rather strict code of never committing a crime there: no horse stealing or cattle theft, no rifling of camps or ranch buildings, despite the fact that no door or gate was ever locked nor a food pantry closed to the needy. In short, it was a haven for shady characters of all kinds, but only if they managed to stay on their best behavior.

The Triangle "camp" of the Crosby gang was apparently just one of many such haunts used by others and was in as isolated a section of that wild country as could be found. Since those days, I have learned that Emmett Dalton once worked for the Bar X Bar, and that while there he met others who later became members of the Dalton gang. These fellows at the time worked for the adjoining Turkey Track outfit south of the Cimarron.

Along about midmorning, Kansas dropped back from where he had shared the lead with Buster to ride alongside me. "Tell me, T.G., why do they call a bunch of Indians the Five Civilized Tribes?

"Because they are, I guess—pretty much civilized. The Chero-kees, Choctaws, Chickasaws, Creeks, Seminoles. Don't you know any history, Kansas? Haven't you heard how those Indians came to Indian Territory? Where they came from?"

"None of that, I reckon," he admitted. "The Indians I knew about back in Texas were mostly Comanches and maybe a few Kiowas. Nobody ever called any of *them* civilized."

"Maybe the Comanches and Kiowas wouldn't call us civilized, either," I replied.

He stared at me. "You an Indian lover, T.G.?"

"No," I said, for once thinking faster than him. "Just a devil's advocate, I guess."

"Oh," he said, clearly wondering what in the world that was. "Well, I was just interested." He quickly spurred on back to his original position alongside Buster.

A smiling Janie pulled up beside me. "You did that nicely, T.G. I'm very proud of you. It's not often any of us manages to best Kansas like that."

"I'm trying to learn those things," I said, working to contain the pride I felt at her compliment. "I figure I better if I'm going to be staying with this gang."

She gave me a searching look. "You sound almost resigned to that."

"Right now, I don't figure I have much choice, do you?"

"Well, not much, I guess. But what I meant was, you don't even seem much bothered by it."

I shrugged. "There's no use being bothered by something unless you can do something about it. At first, I kept thinking I had to get away as soon as possible. Now . . . well, I guess I'm just curious to see what's going to happen next."

"Curious?"

"Sure. I've never been around an outlaw gang before, or on the run, aiming for a hideout in country like this."

She seemed thoughtful. "Will someone be looking for you, T.G.? I don't mean the law or the express company or the railroad people. I mean your family. You do have a family, don't you?"

I frowned. "I have a family, yes. But they've all pretty much moved away from home now. I have no idea if they've heard about what happened to me yet."

"They will eventually, don't you think?"

"Yes. If nothing else, they'll figure something's wrong when I don't write home. Especially my ma. That's been worrying me some, of course."

Janie looked genuinely sympathetic. "Tell me about your family, T.G. Tell me about yourself—how it was with you growing up, things like that."

I told her everything I thought she would be interested in, and found by her questions that she was interested in much more than I had expected. We must have talked twenty minutes about me and my family and my more youthful days, before I finally asked about her.

Somehow I was surprised, although I shouldn't have been, that she wouldn't say much. I gathered from what little she had told me earlier, and again on this occasion, that she and her brothers had come from a respected—though not wealthy—family. Clearly it was Clyde to whom outlawry was so attractive; Buster was almost strictly a follower, and Janie's own tragic experience with a youthful marriage was the principal cause of her involvement. But beyond this, she was very reticent. Partly, I suppose she just didn't want to dredge up any hurtful memories of a young man named Billy Beaumont, but it also must have been just as she said: "You may already know more about us than is good for you to know, T.G. Do you understand what I mean?"

I nodded. "Sure. I can understand why I shouldn't know where you came from in Texas, who your family is there, where you might go if you're ever forced to leave this territory completely. If I'm ever questioned by federal marshals and such, I'm sure I'd be glad not to have to lie to protect you . . ."

She seemed a little surprised at this. "You would do that, T.G.? Lie to protect us?"

"I don't know," I said, not entirely sure myself. "I might, but I really don't know."

This made both of us so thoughtful that we didn't say any more about it after that. We just rode along, either in silence or talking about something else, until just before noon we pulled up at the edge of a clearing half a mile wide and a mile long, with thick woods and hilly slopes all around.

"Well, there it is," Kansas announced, indicating the far end of the clearing. "I figure we came to it pretty good, after all. It's at the edge of those woods up there, beneath those tall trees. Can you see the cabin and corrals there, T.G.? That's our hideout. It's an old cow camp that the Bar X Bar people don't seem to use anymore. What do you think about this for a place to lay low?"

"I don't know," I said. "I haven't ever had to 'lay low' before."

"Well, it's a good spot, take my word for it." And then he peered hard in the direction of the cabin. "I wonder if Clyde and Juice are there yet."

We circled around so we could stay with the woods as we approached the camp, although we needn't have worried about being surprised. Only a small bunch of Bar X Bar cattle—including one monster shorthorn bull—were to be found anywhere close to the house, and they had simply been lying in the shade of a towering walnut that grew near the corrals. The animals jumped up, snorted, and paced off into the brush the moment we rode within sight. Clyde and Juice were not there.

The cabin was built sturdily of logs and had a sod roof that was in serious need of rain to keep its sod from dying. Two stovepipes protruded from the roof. Out back were a set of corrals large enough to hold twenty-five or thirty horses. To one side trickled a small creek, fed, according to my companions, by a cool-water spring located some distance above the corrals. Both the corrals and the cabin were in need of a few repairs but did not really look abandoned. The gang had even left a couple of changes of clothing packed in a crate in one corner of the cabin's main room.

"I figure folks like us have kept it up, such as it is," Kansas informed me as we tied our horses out front. "Come on, have a look around inside."

There were two rooms and half a dozen bunk beds, a cookstove, two kerosene lanterns, a dinner table, cabinets, a rickety food safe (surprisingly not empty, but well stocked with canned goods, flour, salt, sugar, and coffee), a potbellied stove, five hide-backed chairs, and a hat rack by the door with a single well-worn hat hanging from it.

"The food and stuff is all ours," Kansas said as I marveled at both the roominess and the furnishings. "I figure the cookstove was probably heavier than anyone thought it was worth to haul off. We left this place ten days ago with every intention of coming back, as I reckon you already know. What d'you think, T.G.? Will it do?"

I looked at him. "You folks are the outlaws. What I need to know is, do I get a bed?"

Kansas laughed. "That can probably be arranged. Janie gets one room to herself, we get the other. But there's plenty of beds."

Janie walked over to the hatrack and removed the hat. She tossed it to me. "Here, try this on, T.G. Clyde splurged and bought a new one three weeks ago, but you know men — some of them never throw away a hat."

The hat was broad-brimmed and black, dusty and sweat-encrusted. But it fit as well as any I'd ever worn, and I was already looking forward to the relief from the sun it would provide.

Buster and I went out to tend to the horses, while Janie and Kansas began fixing a noon meal. An hour and a half later, after we had eaten, the four of us sat lounging beneath one of the big walnut trees.

After a bit I said to Kansas, "You know, this is all very nice, but I have just one question. What do we do to entertain ourselves while we're here?"

Kansas gave me a sage look. "Well, T.G., that's one thing about this laying low business. Most of the time, it's about as much fun as plucking chickens or scalding hogs."

Mainly, we were there to await Clyde and Juice. They didn't show that day, nor the next, or the next after that. And Kansas was right: It was not a very exciting existence. We could haul water in a bucket from the spring (the creek ran too low at the cabin to be good water), stake the horses out to graze and keep an eye on them while they were doing it, cook and eat meals, or, if we were really ambitious, go out early and late with Kansas to hunt wild turkey, squirrels, or even deer. All of this could account for about three or four of our waking hours if we really stretched things out. After that, it was lay around in the shade and sleep or talk, or maybe just take a walk.

Naturally, I wasn't encouraged to walk alone, or allowed to take the horses out alone, or anything else that might tempt me to escape. By the end of the third day, I had about decided that much more of this and I would be driven to start thinking about getting away all over again.

Of course there was always Janie to keep me interested in hanging around. One morning she even showed up in a dress. She claimed it was the only one she owned and that it had been stashed at the cabin with some of the gang's things when they had been there earlier. On anyone else it might not even have been described as pretty. I recall it as being a solid light blue, ankle-length, high-collared, and long-sleeved. The only break in color or design was a bit of white frill around the neck and wrists.

But it was the first time I had seen Janie in a dress, and I swear she would have made pure burlap the envy of even the fanciest of Sunday-go-to-meeting crowds. It was almost as if she was a different person, and if I hadn't been goofy as a fool over her already, I certainly would've been now.

After supper, that third night, Janie asked if I wanted to walk with her up to the spring. She still wore the dress and had shed the gun belt and six-gun with her other clothes.

"Are you sure you can trust me?" I asked

She looked surprised. "You know, T.G., I didn't even think about that. I guess I just can't think of you as . . . as a prisoner anymore. Should I take my gun?"

"Would you use it on me even if I did try to get away?"

"I believe I once had you thinking I might . . . That seems a long time ago now, doesn't it?"

I smiled. "At least four or five days, I'd say. Was I wrong to think that then? Were you all bluff, or only partly so?"

"I was—and am—a mystery on that score," she said. "So there! Will you walk with me or not?"

Buster and Kansas had taken their chairs outside and sat watching the sun set in a flaming red sky as we stepped past them to begin our walk.

"Does this mean you two are engaged?" Kansas drawled exaggeratedly

Buster was more serious. "You mind your manners with my sister, you hear, messenger?"

I didn't say anything, and Janie only said, "Shut up, you two! Just shut up!"

A well-used trail led through tall grass and beneath all heights of trees in the direction of the spring, parelleling the creek. We passed by the corrals, empty now, as the horses had been staked in the clearing to graze. The creek trickled down the center of the largest corral, which had clearly been built where it was to provide water for animals penned there. This was another reason the creek water at the cabin was no good to us: the animals always got to it first.

Janie wanted to walk slowly, and I was happy to match her pace.

"You won't tell me much about your past," I finally said. "Are we at least allowed to talk about the future?"

"How so? Whose future?"

"Yours," I said simply. "Have you any idea what it will be? Any plans beyond this outlaw life?"

"Why do you want to know that?"

"I'm not sure. Maybe I'm just concerned about you. That's a fault I have. It grows and gets worse the more I get to know and like someone. Maybe I shouldn't say that, but it's true. This business is not right for a girl, and I can't help but wonder what life has in store for you."

She stopped walking and just stared at me, as if I had suddenly revealed an entirely new side of myself. "It hasn't had much at all in store for me so far," she said simply.

"We all have to take our lumps," I pointed out. "It doesn't mean that's all there will ever be."

She wasn't impressed. "You sound so wise, it's as if you were forty and not just—what did you tell me? Nineteen? Twenty?"

"Eighteen," I said. "Why? Do you think I haven't seen my share of things?"

"I don't know. What have you seen? What lumps have you taken?"

We resumed walking. "Well, my pa's death, for one thing. Being kidnapped by outlaws from the first good job I ever had, probably losing that job and maybe being branded an outlaw myself in the process—things like that, I guess."

Again she stopped. "T.G., I'm sorry. I—I forget to think how that must be for you. Will you really lose your job? Do you actually think anyone will believe that newspaper story Kansas showed you?"

I shrugged. "I guess I don't know for sure about the job. The longer I'm gone the less chance I have to return, I'm sure. It may already be too late. As for that story, well, who knows what the people who read it will believe?"

She looked troubled, uncertain.

I said, "Look, don't worry about it. That's what I was trying to tell you a while ago. You have to deal with things the way they are. You have to look ahead. What's done is done. The next thing that happens to you may be the best thing that ever will happen."

"My my!" Her eyes were wide with mock amazement. "You *are* a thinker, aren't you, T.G.? It hardly seems possible that you're no older than me!"

We reached the spring. I don't think it would have amounted to much more than just a muddy seep, except that someone had dug out immediately below it to tap a larger flow. Then they had rock-and-mortar-lined a small collection pool about five feet across by three feet deep, just below the seep. All of this was protected from livestock by a pole fence built just large enough to encompass the spring and collection pool. The pool was clear, overflowing at a rate of approximately ten gallons a minute to feed the creek. A swarm of gnats formed a gray haze in the air.

Janie knelt at the fence and reached between the bottom poles to test the water. "The thing I hate most about this life is being dirty so much. I can't bathe often enough to hardly matter, and I can't keep clean clothes. Even this dress that I only put on yesterday already feel sweaty and dirty."

Swatting gnats, I said, "You deserve better, I sure do think that."

"That's why we're in this business, T.G.," she replied without looking up. "Something better. I thought once that I had found it, the right way. I have nothing to show but bitterness for that. Now, well, my brothers say the right strike, and we can leave the territories. We might go to California, or Oregon, or maybe even somewhere in the East. Any place where we can start anew and forget all that's behind us."

"That sounds like something *you* want," I said. "Are you sure it's what Clyde and Buster want? From what I hear, outlawry gets in the blood. Either that, or the big strike never really comes. What real outlaw gang do you know that's given it up before being run to ground or killed by the law? The James boys, the Youngers? Do you really think even the Daltons will be any different?"

"Clyde says the Daltons are the smartest yet, except maybe for us. He says he'd bet they're in it just the way we are, except they are well known and we're not. When they decide to quit, the rewards will still hang over their heads and they'll have to head for Mexico or South America or some such place. Clyde means it to be different with us. No one will know who we are. We'll just fade away and that will be that."

"You really believe that?" I asked incredulously.

"It's our plan. That's all I know."

"What about me? *I* know who you are."

She looked up. "That's why we can't let you go just yet, T.G. You know that."

"Just *yet*?" I stared at her. "If my knowing who you are is a threat to you, how will you *ever* be able to let me go?"

Again she looked more troubled. "Your questions are too hard for me, T.G. I didn't mean this to turn into a serious talk, so much of it things only Clyde can answer."

"Clyde sure is in charge, isn't he?" I asked, scarcely hiding my disgust. "You'd think he is the smartest man on earth, the way the rest of you kowtow to him."

She seemed to stiffen at this, and her eyes snapped right along with her words. "T.G., I don't want to talk about this anymore. I want to go back now."

"But someone finally has to decide something," I insisted. "This can't just go on forever."

She wheeled on me. "Leave, then. Go ahead, I can't stop you. Just take off." She gave me a withering look, calculated, I suppose, to help me along my way.

I glanced around in exasperation. "You know I can't go anywhere. Not in this wilderness, where I don't know hoot from holler. Not on foot. Why Kansas and Buster would track me down in no time. You know that's no answer."

"Then you'll just have to wait till Clyde gets here," she said icily, and started to walk away.

I let her go about a dozen yards before following suit.

"The way things are," I called after her, "I could be shaving gray whiskers by then."

She neither paused nor looked back.

"Gray whiskers," I repeated, mostly to myself.

CHAPTER 9

AN hour before sundown the next day, two riders appeared in the clearing. I was sitting with Buster and Kansas, watching our horses graze, when we first saw the two men. They came out of the woods and rode generally from west to east, toward us. Janie was preparing supper inside the cabin.

"That's not Clyde and Juice," Kansas said, reaching for his rifle.

"How do you know?" I asked.

"Those aren't their horses. Can't you see? One of them is riding a gray. Neither Clyde nor Juice rode a horse like that."

"Maybe they made a trade or something."

Kansas shook his head. "They might do that, but not for any light-colored horse. Haven't you heard that outlaws only ride dark-colored animals, T.G.?"

"Yes, I guess I've heard that. I never thought too much about whether it was true or not."

"Well, it is. Leastways, far as this gang is concerned, it is. Sure no sense in getting caught by a posse because your horse stands out like a sore thumb in any light, day or night."

"They're coming from the wrong direction, too," Buster observed, shading his eyes with one hand. "I figure Clyde and Juice will come in from the south, and I don't think they'd show themselves like that. Whoever that is sure don't mind us knowing they're coming."

"Why would Clyde and Juice care if we knew?" I asked, feeling dumb but too curious not to ask.

"Because it might not be us. Could be anybody here. They wouldn't take the chance."

The riders drew within a hundred yards of us without stopping. Our horses stood watching curiously, and one of them whinnied.

Janie appeared at the door of the cabin almost instantly upon hearing the horse. She no longer wore her dress, but had once again donned her riding clothes.

"Who are they?" she inquired with a note of concern.

"We don't know yet," Kansas said. "Get back inside and get Buster's rifle. Don't let them see you, but be ready just the same."

Kansas and Buster simply sat in their chairs as if perfectly unconcerned and watched the riders approach.

The twosome rode right up to us but, apparently as a matter of etiquette, did not offer to dismount before being asked to do so. They also seemed wary, and I don't believe I ever saw so many sets of eyes refuse to leave one another at one time. Between Kansas, Buster, and the two newcomers, the intensity of gazes could not be described in words.

Both of the riders seemed tall and leggy, but one was thin and clean-shaven, while the other was almost burly and sported a thick mustache. Not surprisingly, the former was a complete stranger to me. But something about the burly one looked familiar. I was sure I knew the man, or at least had seen him before. I just couldn't remember where or when, and I could not call him by name.

Kansas, his rifle very much in evidence across his lap, was the first to speak. "You fellows Bar X Bar?"

The slender one shook his head. "As it happens, we're not. I don't guess you are either, but we know not to ask names in these parts. Mine's Jordon, though. J. W. Jordon. I have a place about ten miles from here. My friend here is Joe. We're just on our way home. Saw your horses over there, and since we've been looking for some that disappeared about a week ago, we started this way before we realized anyone was here."

Kansas and Buster exchanged looks. "I've heard of you, Jordon," Kansas said. "They call you Cherokee, don't they?"

Jordon's expression did not change. "Yes, some call me that. What else have you heard?"

"Just that you settled here in the Triangle and were one reason the boomers couldn't take over this part of the Strip. Some judge's ruling, wasn't it?"

"Judge Parker at Fort Smith," Jordon allowed easily. "But that was years ago. Before the opening in '89. They'll get this and all the rest eventually. It's just a matter of time."

I sat listening to this with my mouth open and my eyes wide. I too had heard of Jordon. He was supposed to be part Cherokee. I didn't know anything about the legal squabble with the would-be settlers, but I thought it had to do with the boomers' contention that the Cherokees had abandoned this part of the Strip, and thus their claim to it. The presence of Jordon must have been reason enough to prove that they had not. The Bar X Bar people were only tenants there; I guess Jordon was a bonafide resident landowner by virtue of his Indian blood.

"Well," Kansas drawled, "we haven't seen any horses except our own over there. You're welcome to look them over, though; put your minds at ease."

"No need for that," Jordon replied without hesitation. "We can see they're not the ones we're after."

"Were your horses stolen?"

Jordon shared a faint smile with his companion. "We think so, yeah."

"And that doesn't go too well in these parts, does it?"

"Doesn't go well anyplace I've ever been; but yeah, I figure you've heard that we have a special code of sorts hereabouts. We don't ask a man questions about himself; a man doesn't return the favor by stealing or killing while he's here."

"That only seems fair to me," Kansas said. "Too bad someone else didn't think so."

I thought the burly one shifted his weight a bit uneasily at this. I sure did wish I could place the man. I wondered if it could be the mustache, if he was someone I'd known when he was clean-shaven. I tried to imagine him that way.

"Well," Jordon said. "We've still got a fair piece ahead of us tonight. What say we continue on our way, Joe?"

Joe shrugged. "Fine by me."

"You're welcome to get down," Kansas said. "We're expecting to put together a bite of supper soon."

"Thanks," Jordon said. "But I reckon we can't. My people are expecting me home. We'll just be pushing on."

Kansas set his rifle aside and rose. "I hope you'll allow me just one question before you go. This place here—it didn't seem much in use when we found it. You know any reason why we shouldn't stay on for a short spell?"

"A short spell?" Jordon looked thoughtful. "No, I guess I don't know of any such reason. Just if you see any loose horses, you might let me know. I live over that way. Any of the Bar X Bar people can tell you where."

"Sure," Kansas said. "We'll do that. Be glad to."

As we watched them ride away, Kansas said, "Well now, isn't that something! Cherokee Jordon! T.G., do you realize how famous that fellow is in these parts? I wonder who the other fellow was."

"Probably just some saddle bum old Cherokee picked up along the way," Buster speculated knowingly. "Probably nobody more than that."

"You're wrong about that, Buster," I said, finally finding my voice as I watched the two riders disappear in the woods beyond the corrals. "You sure are wrong about that."

Buster gave me a stare. Kansas peered at me suspiciously. Janie reappeared at the doorway of the cabin, probably wondering if it would do for her to come out now.

"It took me a while," I said. "The mustache threw me. But believe me, that saddle bum of yours, Buster, is easily more famous than Mr. Cherokee Jordon ever thought about being. His name is Gratton, Grat for short. And he is the older brother of Emmett and Bob Dalton, who you and Clyde so poorly imitated back near Leliaetta better than a week ago!"

We had no idea what Grat Dalton had been doing with Jordon. Years later, I read a tale claiming that once, while fleeing a posse, the Dalton gang had presumed to take some of Jordon's horses as replacements for their own exhausted mounts. It was a Triangle *faux pas* of the first order. Upon receiving threats from Jordon that if the horses were not returned he would personally lead the law to them, the Daltons soon made sure the horses found their way home. Or so the story goes. I have no idea if such a thing ever happened; I have even less of an idea if Grat Dalton's presence that day with Jordon had anything to do with horse theft at all. I really think it more likely they were just checking us out. But one thing I do know: The incident sure made Kansas and Buster nervous, especially since now one more day had passed without a sign of Clyde or Juice.

"I don't know how long we can stay here like this," Kansas remarked after supper that night. "Clyde and Juice should have been here by now."

Buster shook his head. "Grat Dalton. Dammit, T.G., are you sure that's who that fellow was?"

"It was Grat Dalton, all right," I said. We were sitting once more in front of the cabin, watching the faint last light of day disappear from the sky and listening to crickets chirp. "I just don't know how I took so long to figure him out, even with the mustache."

Janie came out of the cabin to join us. She brought her chair with her but did not set it down beside me. I guess I was still in the doghouse from the night before.

"Does it mean anything?" she asked. "Those two men coming here like that?"

"I doubt it," Kansas said. "From everything I've ever heard about Jordon, he's straight with what he says, especially that part about the code. Dalton, well, he's in the same boat we're in — dodging marshals and sheriffs; he should be no threat to another outlaw."

"Wouldn't it have been something if Clyde had been here?" Buster marveled. "As much as he thinks of the Daltons, wouldn't it though!"

"Why *isn't* Clyde here, Kansas?" Janie asked. "It's already been at least two days longer than you told us it would be."

"I don't know," Kansas worried. "I just sure don't know."

We didn't talk any more about it. The horses were still grazing in the clearing, and presently Kansas and Buster decided to corral them for the night. Janie and I were left to ourselves to watch the stars twinkle and hear the crickets chirp. We hadn't said six words to each other all day.

Finally I decided to effect a break in the silence. "I'm sorry about last night. I didn't mean to make you mad."

She sighed. "You only made me mad at myself, T.G. You shouldn't have to apologize. You were right in everything you said, and I just wasn't prepared to deal with it. I guess I wasn't really mad at you at all.

"You sure *seemed* mad at me," I said. "you've seemed that way all day."

"Then it's me who should apologize. I've just been worried about Clyde, and what we talked about last night only made me worry more. Clyde's always where he says he'll be when he says he'll be there. Nothing like this has happened before."

"Maybe Juice had complications. Maybe the doctor really did have to amputate his foot."

She didn't seem much convinced of this.

"You think maybe the law caught up to them? Something like that?"

"I don't want to think that, no. But of course I can't help allowing for the possibility. I just wish we knew, that's all."

"Maybe Kansas could go look for them. Ingalls isn't so far from here, is it?"

She shrugged. "If they don't come soon, that is a thought, I guess."

Again we lapsed into silence, just sitting there, our chairs several feet apart. We heard Buster and Kansas talking as they led the horses toward the corrals. In the sky, to the northwest, a cloud bank had appeared and was blotting out the stars there. Lightning flickered among the clouds. At last Janie rose from her chair.

"I think I'll turn in. It's been a do-nothing day, but I'm still tired."

"Yeah," I agreed, but did not offer to follow her lead. "I'll just wait for Buster and Kansas. They should be along shortly."

"Good night, then," she said, and carrying her chair with her, disappeared through the cabin door. A few minutes later, the lantern in her room went out, and I sat alone with only a doorway patch of light furnished by the remaining lantern in the main room to break the darkness.

I got to thinking how easy it would be to just get up and walk away. They had come to trust me so that only at times did it even occur to them to take precautions against my escaping. Usually this still had to do with my being left alone with the horses or a gun, but even at night in the cabin I was not guarded. I could slip away nearly anytime. Why didn't I do it? I had advanced a number of reasons to myself previously, all very practical, very real. But were they reason enough? Now that I had the gang lulled into hardly watching me, why not just go ahead and make my break?

I guess it sort of boiled down to my feelings for Janie; everything else was an excuse. I felt stupid admitting that, even to myself, but I guess I couldn't ignore the truth altogether. Talk about a lovesick calf! What future could I possibly think I might have with this outlaw girl? Even if she should come to feel about me the way I did about her, could we ever be married? I would then have not only an outlawed girl for a wife, but outlawed *inlaws* to boot!

My thoughts were becoming incongruous; I was ashamed of

them, and almost felt like getting up and just walking away right then. But I didn't have the chance, for I heard Buster and Kansas coming back from the corrals. I turned just as they came into the lamplight.

"Come on, T.G.," Kansas said. "It's bedtime. Gotta get a good night's sleep so we can get up and do more of this tomorrow."

"Yeah, T.G., ain't this an exciting life?" Buster chimed in.

I rose from my chair. "Makes me wonder why you fellows don't just work for a living. Seems to me, cutting fence posts for sodbusters would beat this."

"Haw haw haw," Buster carried on as he followed me inside. "Haw haw haw."

I was awakened an hour or two later by a tremendous crash of thunder. I found myself sitting upright in my bunk, heart pounding, trying to see in a room of pure darkness. A few feet away, Buster must have been doing the same thing, for I heard him breathing hard from his own bunk. Kansas slept near the door; I couldn't tell if he was awake or not.

"Did you hear that, T.G.?" Buster asked. "Damn! If our roof don't get wet tonight, it never will!"

Lightning flashed, briefly illuminating the room. I saw someone standing in the doorway.

"Kansas? Is that you?"

"Yeah, it's me. Some storm, ain't it? You boys scared of storms?"

"What d'you mean scared?" Buster asked. "You're the one that's out of bed."

"It's not the storm that got me out." More lightning flickered and I thought I heard a few tentative raindrops begin to splatter on the stovepipes in the roof. "I thought I heard a horse nicker a minute or so ago. I don't think it was one of ours."

"How in hell can you tell *that*?" Buster asked.

"It didn't come from the corrals. I figure someone's out there."

I heard what I thought were Buster's stockinged feet hit the floor, and what I knew was a curse. "Dammit, where are my boots?"

I too swung my legs over the edge of my bunk, but then I only sat there, unsure what I would do if I got up. I decided to at least put on my pants, for I slept in my underwear, and it was a good thing I did. No sooner was I finished with this than I heard Janie's voice at the door to the other room.

"What is it?" she asked sleepily, yet still with some alarm. "What's all the talking about?"

"Kansas thinks someone's outside," Buster told her. "Best keep your gun handy till we find out for sure."

Lightning once again framed Kansas in the doorway; thunder clapped so hard it shook the house. "Well, I'll be damned," Kansas drawled. "I sure will be damned!"

"What is it?" Janie asked.

"Company," he said. "You'll be glad to know who. Buster, fire up a lantern, will you? Come on, be quick!"

No more had Buster fumbled around and done this than two dark-hatted forms appeared at the doorway. It was Clyde and Juice, the former looking somewhat overburdened by a saddle in each hand, a rifle under one arm, and a pair of saddlebags slung over one shoulder. Juice carried almost nothing and hobbled with the use of a cane. Clyde let the saddlebags slide from his shoulder to the floor.

"Clyde!" It was Janie. "Where on earth have you been?"

"Well, little sister, we got just a bit sidetracked. We wandered up to a little burg south of the Cimarron and found ourselves a little business there . . ."

"South of the Cimarron? A little business? *What* business?"

He smiled expansively. "Why eight hundred dollars worth and a packsaddle full of supplies, that's what! We robbed a general store and then blew a safe at the post office, both in the same night. Can you believe that—both in one night?"

Buster, Kansas, Janie, and I exchanged looks all around. Astounded was hardly the word for how I'm sure the other three felt. It was easily the word for my reaction. Buster, I think, was most affected of all.

"Oh, for chrissake, Clyde. A *post office?*"

CHAPTER 10

THE two men shed still-dry raincoats and their saddles were dumped in the corner of the room. Outside, what had been till then only scattered raindrops suddenly became a downpour. Janie ducked back inside her room to get more clothes on, while the rest of us pulled up chairs to watch Clyde dump the contents of one saddlebag on the table. Everything from gold coin to paper poured out.

"We unloaded our pack and packsaddle by the corrals," Clyde told us. "The pack is tarp-covered, so the rain shouldn't hurt things. We've got food and supplies for two weeks in there, all from the general store we robbed. Dammit, Buster, you and Kansas should've been there! We really pulled it off slick. If it hadn't been for having to blow the safe at the post office, hell, I bet we'd never even have been chased—"

"Wait a minute!" Kansas broke in suddenly. "What do you mean 'chased'?"

Janie came into the room and plopped down on the end of Buster's bunk to listen, all the chairs having been taken.

Clyde looked at Kansas. "Chased? I should say. Why, I figure we had at least two posses after us for a while. But we handled it slick, fellows, I mean real slick. Just let me tell it the way it happened, okay?"

Everyone more or less nodded, and Clyde drew a breath. "After Kansas left us at Ingalls, me and Juice just hung around for a couple of days to give Juice's foot time to get a little better. The doc finally admitted Juice wasn't gonna lose the damn thing and gave him medicine for the pain. So, after those two days, we started out to come straight here. But then we got to thinking: We knew we'd soon need more supplies and probably a packhorse. We didn't want to go back to Ingalls, and wanted even less to show ourselves anyplace else close by—just as a precaution, you understand. So I said to Juice, why pay good money for something when we didn't have to? Why not hold up a store? We could take what supplies we need and what money was laying around as well. Why not?

"Well, Juice's foot was just enough of a slow-down to make us think twice about an out-and-out holdup. Just the slightest problem, and he might not be able to move quick enough to get away. So we decided to go somewhere and break in at night. Only we didn't want to do it near here; we wanted plenty of territory between us and this camp. So we rode west. We found this little old town just made to order. We rode in, looked things over real good, noticed the post office, and left out again. We camped two miles out of town in a brushy bottom to wait for a good hour.

"About midnight, we rode back in. You never saw a town so fast asleep. We stole a horse at the livery stables, went over to the general store and broke in the back way by picking a padlock, fitted ourselves out right proper with packsaddle, grub, and gear, and loaded our new packhorse up out back. Then we rifled the till, took a good-sized charge of dynamite, and went over to the post office. We broke in the back way just like at the store, and while Juice held the horses, I blew and cleaned out the safe. Damn, it was slick! Of course, we woke up that whole sorry little town when the safe blew. But we were in the saddle and on our way in no time. And look here on the table. Eight hundred smackaroos and then some! What d'you think, gang? Is this okay or isn't it?"

The gang just looked at one another. I certainly had never heard Clyde talk so much, and I'm not sure his brother or sister had, either.

"Tell them, Juice," Clyde said. "Tell them how slick it was."

Juice looked as if he felt coached. "It was slick, all right. Real slick."

"How's your foot, Juice?" Kansas asked.

"The doc wrapped it good, and the painkiller works pretty good. I stole me some new boots at that general store, but I can't wear 'em yet." His expression seemed to say this was about as optimistic a report as he was able to give at the moment. As if to prove it, he added, "God damn sore and swole up is how it is, mostly."

Kansas turned back to Clyde, eyes narrowed. "The posses, Clyde. Tell us about that part. Did you lose them or not?"

Clyde's expression clouded slightly. "Somebody in that little town must have put a bunch of men together fast that night. We rode about fifteen miles and stopped to rest about daybreak. Four hours later we saw them coming about two miles away, in open country. We sneaked away in a wooded bottom, but it took us most of the day to give them the slip. It rained that night and I guess wiped out our tracks, at least enough to fool that bunch. They weren't much of a posse, I guess."

"And the other one? You said there were two."

"Well, that was a little closer a call," Clyde admitted somewhat reluctantly. "I guess someone telegraphed ahead of us, probably to Guthrie. We were almost intercepted south of Orlando by another posse. Lucky for us, we saw them first again and were able to slip away. We led them northeastward and I figure lost them before we came anywhere near the Triangle. It's rained behind us twice now, not counting tonight, so I'm hoping we gave them the slip as well."

Kansas looked a bit skeptical. "And your horses? What kind of shape are they in?"

"Not the best. Fact is, they're pretty done in. But none of them is ruined. They'll be okay with a few days rest and a chance to fill their bellies with good grass. No problem on that score." He truly did not seem worried about anything.

"So what are the plans, Clyde?" Janie wanted to know. "What do we do from here?"

"Why, we hole up here for a spell. That's been the plan all along; you know that."

"After that, Clyde. I mean, what's next after that?"

For perhaps the first time since the discussion began, Clyde's eyes settled briefly on me. Then he looked back at his sister. "I'm working on something, another job. I, uh, don't reckon I'm ready yet to say just what kind, though." Again, he glanced over at me.

I straightened in my chair. "If you want me to leave so you can talk freely, I will."

Clyde almost smiled. "No, that won't be necessary. I'll tell everyone in due time, you included, messenger. No point in worrying about it now."

I straightened, looked around, took a deep breath. "If you don't mind, I'd like to worry about at least some of it now. The part that has to do with me, at least. By my reckoning, I've spent eight days and almost nine nights as a captive of this gang now, damn near all of it waiting for you and you alone to decide what's going to be done with me. Seems to me you've had time maybe to do that by now."

Clyde's look of surprise, I believe, was completely genuine. He leaned back in his chair and just stared at me. Finally he said, "Kansas, didn't you show our friend here that newspaper story? Didn't he read it?"

"He read it."

Clyde said to me, "They think you're one of us, messenger. They think you were our inside man."

"That was just a newspaper story," I said. "No one will believe it when the truth comes out. When I'm back and can tell what really happened, they'll know it wasn't true."

He actually laughed—much longer and much louder than I thought appropriate. But then his eyes narrowed as he leaned forward and looked straight at me. His seriousness bothered me much more than his mirth.

"I think you just stated our problem pretty well, friend messenger. The way it is now, folks either don't know who we are or they think our jobs were done by the Daltons. They may or may not know what to think about you. The situation is, we want to keep it that way. That means we can't have you going around telling people what 'really happened.' That's why we took you in the first place and that's why we've got to keep you. It's either that or shoot you, whichever you choose. I regret the necessity of that, but such is life. Do you understand what I'm saying?"

I sighed. "You don't offer me much hope, Clyde. And you sure don't seem to be seeing things from my point of view. I mean, really, what is the solution for me? When will you ever be willing to let me go?"

He met my gaze straight on, I have to give him that, and his eyes were steely blue. "Look, messenger—hell, why do I keep calling you that? What's your name, anyway?" It seemed strange, after all this time, but I guess he had been gone so much of it he really didn't know.

"T.G. They call me T.G."

"Okay, T.G. I'll say it as straight as I know how. We're in this for the big money, and I do mean big. One job or half a dozen, whatever it takes. When we've accomplished that, we're through. We don't want fame, and we only want so much excitement. Accept that if you can; if you can't, well, that's your problem. The point is, now this thing has happened and there's nothing any of us can do to change it, and if you value your health at all, you're in it with us until our goal is reached. I'm sorry about that, but it's the best I can do.

"Now, when we're done with this business, when we're ready to quit—and the sooner the better, too—Kansas and Juice will go their way, and my sister, my brother, and me will go ours. We aim to go just as far away as we can get; we plan to change our identities; and we *don't* plan on ever being found out by the law. I can't promise you a damn thing, not now at least. You know who we are, and it'll depend on the circumstances, and on you, what we do with you. Maybe we'll turn you loose, who knows? You won't know where we're going, and we'll never again use our true names. Maybe even if you do tell your story, it won't matter. Maybe by then you won't be any freer to talk to the law than we would be. Scoff at that newspaper story if you will, folks are gonna believe it. You're gonna be an outlaw just like us."

I guess I just stared at him. I couldn't believe what I'd just heard.

"Okay, T.G., have *you* got a solution?"

"Well, if I promise not to tell anyone who you are, would you let me go now?"

He at least did me the honor of not laughing at this. "In my place, would you do that?"

"No. No, I guess I wouldn't."

I must have looked pretty chagrined, for Clyde said, "Aw, come on, T.G., don't look like that. I'm not a bad sort, really. Hell, I'm even beginning to like you, boy. And since you know those Daltons, why, you might even be of some help to us with our disguises and such. What do you think about that?"

"Yeah," Buster put it. "And just remember. It was those Daltons who got you into this. If you hadn't known what they looked like . . ." Suddenly he paused. "Clyde, by golly, we haven't told you the latest on that. Did you know we had a visit from Grat Dalton just this afternoon?"

Clyde, if he never perked up at anything, sure perked up at this.

Over the next day or so, I began thinking again that I would just have to escape. It wasn't going to be easy, because now that Clyde was back the vigilance of the gang was no longer so relaxed. This was especially true after that little talk of ours on the night of his arrival. I'm sure they knew what I would have in mind after that.

One thing I was *not* going to do: try to grab a gun and shoot my way out. I had done enough fool things in may life not to pull something like that with five perfectly authentic outlaws there to stop me. Well, four, anyway. I could hardly count Janie in that category, but then, as she had warned me more than once, I really couldn't count her out of it either. Even she didn't know for sure, but she *might* shoot. I figure she deserved at least some caution on that score.

Mostly, I had to admit that Clyde was no fool. He did not insist that I be tied up in my bunk at night, but he nightly pulled his own bunk over to a spot square in front of the door. He also had those of Kansas and Buster parked beneath the only two windows in the room. He had everyone sleep with both their handguns and rifles close at hand; and he explained to me that any attempt on my part to escape would be a good way to get myself killed. During the day, I was to be watched by someone at all times. As before, I was never to be allowed near the horses alone, nor to handle a gun.

Other than this slightly increased vigilance, however, my daily relationship with the gang remained pretty much the same as it had been when only Kansas, Buster, and Janie were in charge. I thought if I would just be patient, if I would just give the right opportunity a chance to come, sooner or later I would get away and bring the adventure to an end.

That's what I thought late in the month of June, that summer of 1892.

Kansas and Buster found some wooden crates out behind the cabin and spent a lot of time one morning fashioning traps for quail, of which there seemed to be plenty around. We had no shotgun, however, and with rifles we either couldn't hit birds that size or blew them to pieces when we did. The traps were the only good way to go. Kansas claimed to know all about how to make and set the things; Buster simply claimed to relish fried quail.

Janie and I watched them at their task for perhaps half an hour that morning, then Janie suggested we go for a walk in the woods and maybe collect some firewood for the cookstove. It had rained twice since Clyde's arrival at camp, and dry wood was at a premium. Standing dead oak was what we looked for, and I carried an ax along while Janie somewhat pointedly carried Buster's rifle.

"Maybe I'll see a deer," she told me as we left the cabin.

"Or a damned fool former messenger trying to get away," I replied dryly. "I know, Janie, I know."

"I wish you wouldn't keep saying those things, T.G." We were walking past the corrals where Clyde and Juice were replacing a horseshoe thrown just the day before by Clyde's horse. "I feel bad enough already about you."

"Where are you two going?" Clyde called out as he saw us about to pass. He had been bent over, the horse's left front foot raised and held between his knees as he reset the shoe. Juice was mainly watching as Clyde worked with hammer and rasp. Clyde stopped what he was doing and came to meet us at the corral fence.

"We're going after some firewood," Janie told hime. "Don't worry, we won't go far. Everything will be all right."

"You just make sure it is," he warned. "Especially you, T.G. Remember, you can't get as far on foot around here as I can spit. Don't do anything stupid."

I promised I would not.

We were barely out of sight of the corrals and the cabin when I said, "You realize we can't carry very much wood by hand, don't you?"

"I know," Janie replied. "That's not really why I wanted to come anyway."

"Oh?"

She pointed toward a stand of trees. "Over there, a dead blackjack. Let's cut that one while we talk."

I shrugged and followed her over to the tree. It stood maybe fifteen feet tall and looked very stark among its green-leaved brethren. I measured it with my eye and hefted the ax. It took four good strokes, two on opposite sides, to make it ready to fall. I gave it a push and watched it topple. Janie watched from one side as I went to work stripping branches.

She looked contemplative as she said, "Tell me, T.G. I mean truthfully. Do you think me bad, because of what I am—me and my brothers? This gang?"

I straightened from my task. "Are you serious?"

"Yes, I am. I really want to know."

"Well," I said, thinking about it, "I don't think you bad. Foolish maybe, poorly advised, but not bad."

"Do you think anything else about me?"

"Yes . . . I do. I think you pretty, very pretty, maybe the prettiest girl I ever met. I think that for sure."

For a moment she just stared at me. Then she looked down at herself. "Even like this? In a man's shirt and pants and wearing a gun? You think me pretty, even like this?"

"Of course, I do," I said. "Besides, this is not the only way I've seen you. I . . ." My voice failed me. I had spoken without thinking, only just in time to stop myself as I recalled that moonlight vision I would never forget of her on a remote creek bank in Osage country. I couldn't have finished my sentence if someone had given it to me to read.

At first she looked quizzical, then she said, "Oh, you must mean the dress. Was that it? *That* old thing?"

I gulped. "Why, yes . . . the dress. I . . . thought it was very attractive on you . . . ." Something made me pause as her eyes searched mine. It was as if she was seeing something she didn't want to see. Her voice was very low as she said, "T.G., I don't want you to fall in love with me. Whatever else happens, I don't want that."

I didn't know what to say. I guess I just stood their gawking.

"I'm serious, T.G. It would only mean trouble and unhappiness for both of us. Believe me, it would."

"Look, Janie, I know you think you're doing me a favor, here, but—"

"I'm a member of an outlaw gang, T.G. I've been married. I—"

Somehow this irritated me. "So what are you—spoiled fruit? Is your life over because of those things? Is that what you're saying?"

She shook her head. "No . . . no, that's not it at all. I'm saying that I'm no good for you, T.G. Whether you know it or not, you would be better off if you had never laid eyes on me. That's what I'm saying."

"And you don't think I can decide something like that for myself? You think I'm just a kid or something?"

"I didn't say that—"

"Would it be different if I were Kansas or Juice? An outlaw too? Would that make a difference?"

"You are *not* Kansas or Juice, T.G.! Don't you say that! Don't you even think it!"

I stared at her, my mind churning. She didn't know the half of the way I felt. I couldn't be mad at her for what she said, even if I wanted to. I wanted so badly to reach out and touch her, to hold her, to kiss her, that I almost couldn't think of anything else. Good thing I was still holding the ax, I guess. It gave me something to squeeze.

Finally I said, "I'll think and do what I want, Janie. You can't change that."

She didn't reply. She just looked almost helplessly at me, and a while later, when we had collected all the firewood we could carry, we made our way on back to the cabin. Neither of us was angry, but for the second time in forty-eight hours, I doubt that we said a half a dozen words to each other throughout the balance of a day.

CHAPTER 11

THE days were muggy and hot, so much so that the sweat poured off us. Even the nights were hot, and almost everything we touched seemed soggy. On what we calculated to be the first day of July, Kansas and Buster grew so restless they decided to make a trip to either Ingalls or Pawnee (then called the Pawnee Agency) for a night or two on the town. Clyde didn't seem terribly happy about the idea, but I suppose he figured the two of them could only be kept under control for so long anyway, and in the name of harmony he finally agreed to let them go.

"Just watch your step, you hear?" he told them as they mounted up to ride out that morning. It seemed we were always needing more supplies, so they were taking a packhorse with them. This time, however, they would pay for what they brought; nothing was to be done to turn even the slightest suspicion of the law their way.

We were all there to watch them ride away—Clyde, Janie, Juice, and me—and when they were out of sight, Juice hobbled over to his chair in front of the cabin and sat down.

"What this place needs is a porch," he grumped. "And a bathtub. Dammit, I'm sick of being smelly with sweat all the time."

We had started going to the creek just below the spring in the evenings to take what I guess you could call sponge baths—the men at one time, Janie—alone, of course—at another. We would strip and wash down with wash rags, trying to at least cool ourselves off and get rid of the sweat. It was about the best we could do, really. We weren't about to bathe in the spring's catchment pool (our only source of drinking water), and the creek farther down was little more than a fetid dribble.

"Is your foot bothering you again, Juice?" Janie asked. "Sometimes the way you act, it almost seems as if it's getting worse."

"That's because I figure it *is* getting worse," he said. "That damned doc—all he wanted to do was amputate. Son of a gun probably got his training in the Yankee army during the war and hasn't learned a stinking thing since."

"Maybe you ought to let us have a look at it," she suggested. It was something he had been unwilling to do ever since he had arrived at the camp with Clyde a week ago. The only obvious thing was that the foot had remained far too swollen for him to get a boot over it. He kept it wrapped and used his cane, hobbling with the foot off the ground to keep the bandaging as clean as possible.

He just shook his head. "Nothing you could do. I take my medicine and doctor it just the way the doc said. Can't nothing more be done."

This wasn't exactly true. He had a bottle of whiskey he had been using to supplement the doc's prescriptions. We doubted this was helping things any, but there was no telling Juice that.

Janie turned to me. "Would you bring a bucket of water from the spring, T.G.? I've got breakfast dishes to wash yet."

I looked at Clyde. He shrugged. "Go ahead. I'll be over at the corrals. You couldn't get far if you wanted to."

I went to get the bucket while Clyde headed for the corrals. Janie went back inside the cabin and Juice just sat in his chair.

A few minutes later I passed by the corrals, where Clyde seemed to be doing nothing in particular except maybe looking the horses over. It seemed strange, but I hadn't thought much about escaping for the past day or so. A good chance just had not presented itself. I wondered more and more, though, about my ma and whether she knew yet what had happened to me. My brothers and sisters would be worried about me too. Eventually, if I didn't get free of the gang, maybe I could at least get word home—a letter, somehow. I had no idea how I would manage that; it did make me feel better to have thought of it, however.

I filled my bucket at the spring and started back. As I passed back by the corrals, Clyde called to me. "Come here a minute, T.G. I want to ask you something."

I walked up to the fence and set the bucket down.

Clyde ambled over to stand just across from me. "I've been meaning to ask you: Are you absolutely positive that fellow you saw here with Cherokee Jordon was Grat Dalton?"

"As positive as I've been about anything lately."

"Yet you've no idea what he was doing here."

I shrugged. We had been over this before. "They said they were hunting some horses that had gotten either lost or stolen. Other than that, I suspect Dalton has been lying low just like you are. Remember, that gang is not only wanted, its members are known by a lot of people. It has to be harder for them than it is for you just because of that."

"They've also got friends everywhere," Clyde pointed out. "People who will both lie for them and hide them whenever the law approaches. We're not known, but we don't have those kinds of friends, either."

"Maybe so," I said, not sure I really cared.

But Clyde was not through thinking about it. "I wonder if his brothers were around someplace. Them or maybe Doolin or Pierce or others of the gang. I wonder what job they'll pull next. It's been a month now since Red Rock. Maybe we just haven't had a chance to hear yet about anything new."

Sometimes Clyde could get really tiresome on this subject. "You sure are taken with this Dalton stuff, Clyde. What are they, your heroes?"

"Maybe they are, I don't know. So what? They're a gutsy outfit. I admire that. In my business, wouldn't you?"

I somewhat grudgingly allowed that I might.

"Besides, you know how we're operating. It's important that we know all we can about the Daltons. Very important."

"Going around impersonating your heroes could get them in just that much more trouble, you know. Doesn't that bother you?"

"Better them than us, I always say."

I eyed him thoughtfully. "Have you decided on your next job yet? You said a week ago you were working on a plan."

His gaze was quickly suspicious. "Now, wouldn't you like to know that. Wouldn't you now!" But then as I bent to pick up my water bucket and started to leave, he sort of grinned and asked, "T.G., tell me, how would you like to become a bank robber?"

I gaped at him. "That's it? A bank? You're going to rob a bank?"

He wouldn't tell me straight out. He just laughed and said, "It might beat robbing post offices. It sure might do that!"

The Fourth of July rolled around, and Kansas and Buster still weren't back. We probably wouldn't have celebrated much anyway, but Clyde was in an especially nonfestive mood.

"I told you what would happen," Janie remarked over our noon meal. "There's no way they'll miss a chance to celebrate a holiday."

"Yeah, yeah, I know," Clyde conceded. "They just damn well better be back by tomorrow night, that's all."

About two o'clock, Clyde and I staked the horses out to graze in the clearing. Because of recent rains, the grass there was green and growing at a rate that four grazing horses could scarcely hope to keep up with.

An hour or so later, clouds began to build. Initially, they promised little more than to blot out the sun and cool things down a bit. Juice had hobbled to a place up the creek where he could soak his foot. Clyde was taking a nap on his bunk inside the cabin. I was off to one side of the cabin inspecting a couple of Kansas's quail traps, idle now while their builder was away. Janie sat on a nearby log, I guess mostly keeping watch on me.

After a bit, Janie looked out across the clearing and asked, "T.G., where is Juice's horse?"

I looked up. "What do you mean? Isn't he there with the others?" One corner of the cabin blocked my view; I couldn't see any of the horses from where I stood.

"I see Clyde's, mine, and that bay of yours. But not Juice's sorrel."

I came over to where she sat. "He's probably just lying down. From here you'd never see him in that tall grass."

"That's probably it, all right," she agreed a bit tentatively. Depending on where the animals stood, sometimes only their backs could be seen over the grass anyway.

Nonetheless, we both continued to watch the clearing. It seemed strange that any of the horses would lie down after having been turned out to graze only a short while before. The other three animals were actively grazing.

"I guess we could walk over there and see," I suggested.

It was about a hundred and fifty yards to the nearest horse. We followed a cow trail through the grass. Clumps of armpit-high bluestem and Indiangrass brushed at our arms and legs as we walked. Janie said, "If those clouds keep building, it can't help but rain."

I looked skyward. "You're probably right about that."

The horses were accustomed to being approached directly while staked and did not spook as we walked up to them. My bay and Juice's sorrel had been located on past the other two. The bay actually nickered as I approached; the sorrel should have been just beyond.

"He isn't there," Janie said. "He isn't lying down."

I had to look some in the grass to find the animal's stake pin; there was no sign of its rope and the only signs of the horse were a couple of dung piles and a good deal of trampled or partially eaten grass.

We both looked around, as far as we could see in every direction. The horse was not in sight.

"Who tied him?" Janie asked.

"I'm afraid I did. I tied my bay and Juice's sorrel; Clyde did the other two."

"I was afraid of that," she moaned.

I looked around some more. "You wouldn't think he would wander far. Maybe he'll come back on his own after a while."

"Well, I suppose there is that chance, all right."

I began studying the ground beyond the animal's grazing perimeter. "Maybe we could track him. He may not have gone far."

"That's possible," Janie said. "But I would suggest we saddle our horses and ride after him. We might or might not do any good on foot."

"Should we wake Clyde and tell him first?"

She looked toward the cabin. "I don't think that's going to be a choice we have. Here he comes now."

I followed her gaze. Clyde had just left the cabin and was striding our way. He probably already suspected that something was up.

"I feel just like I used to when my pa would come after me with a strap," I said.

Fortunately, Clyde didn't have a strap, just an acid tongue. I wasn't prepared to take very much off him, but by the same token I could see why he was so unquestionably the boss of the gang. Fortunately again, he was more concerned with going after the horse than he was with quarreling overlong with me.

"Well, come on," he told us after looking around at the tracks. "If we're going to find that nag, we'll have to do it before it rains and wipes out the tracks. T.G. and I will go. Janie, you go ahead and put your horse in the corral. You and Juice can watch the cabin while we're gone."

Janie left to do as she was told while Clyde and I went on over to the cabin to saddle up. Juice was there by the time we arrived and was no more happy to learn what had happened than Clyde had been.

"Here I am," he grumped, "the one man who can't afford to be put on foot, and you let *my* horse get away."

"I'm sorry, Juice," I said. "I don't know how that knot could have come loose. I really don't."

Clyde and I had our horses saddled and were preparing to mount by the time Janie arrived back from the corrals. The sky was almost completely overcast by then, and one could see blue curtains of rain stretching toward the ground to the southwest.

"We're going to have to hurry," Clyde said. "Come on, T.G., mount up."

The missing horse's tracks indicated that the animal had entered the woods going in a northerly direction and was probably not in a hurry. Most likely, he had grazed his way along until he had, more by accident than anything else, left the clearing and worked his way beyond our view in the woods.

"He's probably not that far away," Clyde said as I followed along behind him. "It's just that these trees are so thick we'll have to track him down to find him."

That our time in which to accomplish this was growing short was now obvious. The sky had continued to darken and the wind had begun to pick up to the point that Clyde and I almost had to shout to hear one another. Already I had begun to feel windblown drops of rain against my face.

The horse's tracks veered eastward, following a cow trail. Clyde's horse moved comfortably at a rapid walk, which left my shorter-legged bay having to trot to keep up. But for the trail, which I knew I could follow all the way back to the clearing, I think I would have been over half lost already.

We went about a mile like this, and somewhere along the way Clyde began to outdistance me. Once or twice, he called for me to keep up, but generally I think he had a tendency to forget about me in favor of concentrating on the tracks he was following.

The rain continued mostly to spit with the wind. I was beginning to wish I had brought a jacket along. The temperature drop of the past half hour was almost unbelievable. Already beginning to shiver, I could imagine how it was going to be if a soaking rain were to come.

Which it did, with the characteristic suddenness of an Oklahoma downpour, just at the time when Clyde hollered something back at me about having sighted the missing horse and then disappeared behind a large growth of brush.

At first it never occurred to me to do anything but follow along, and that is just what I tried to do. But when I rounded the brush clump, there was no sign of Clyde. I pulled up in a sheet of rain. You wouldn't believe how quickly a downpour like that can wash tracks away. I tried to find some, and a little farther on even thought I could see where a hoof had slid in the mud. But Clyde had abandoned the cow trail at that point, and lacking anything more to go on than that one hoofprint, I simply couldn't tell where he had gone.

I started to call out to him; I even had my hands cupped to my mouth to do so. But then I thought: What are you doing? After all this time waiting for your chance to get away, what on earth are you doing?

I looked around. The rain seemed to pour even harder. Lightning struck a tree twenty-five yards to my right with a deafening crack. In the midst of my shock from this, my horse shied and almost dumped me; I grabbed leather and was not one bit ashamed for having done so. Even at that, I barely managed to hang on. The smell of ozone was strong in the air. A tremendous clap of thunder seemed to shake the earth. My horse, back under control in only the most tentative way, trembled beneath me.

Water poured from the brim of my hat. Lightning flashed and struck again some distance away. I had a distinct urge to get out in the open, away from the trees.

I kicked the horse forward, in a direction I thought was back toward the clearing. I don't know how far I rode before finally admitting to myself that I must have missed the mark. All I found were more trees. Water was running everywhere and the ground has turned to slick, sticky mud. I couldn't locate Clyde and was very unsure where *I* was. I rode on, feeling quite lost.

Finally the rain let up. By then, I was so soaked and cold and miserable that I hardly cared. I craved shelter and dry clothes and maybe a fire to sit beside. I had none of these, and even if I had been trying to return to camp, I'm not sure I could have located it.

Everything was wet; even after the rain had stopped completely, I was still getting slapped at almost every turn by branches laden with water. I was miserable, and yet in one way I felt good. For the first time in days and days, I was no longer a prisoner. And it had all happened so simply, so easily.

I wondered if Clyde was looking for me. How soon had he missed me? How far had I come after we were separated?

I kept riding. The sun broke through the clouds, and it was in my face. I had somehow swung around and was going west. I felt better and better. Sunset was only an hour or so away, but I didn't give a thought to what I would do overnight. I had no food, no bedroll, no jacket, no matches, no gun. But I had gotten away. The more I thought about it, the more exhilarated I became. I had no plans except to keep going, to eventually find a town, a place where I could tell someone who I was and what had happened to me. . . .

I thought of Janie. My exhilaration eased. I tried to be practical. The girl represented something I would have to put behind me. She would be a nice memory, no more. I tried very hard to convince myself that I could handle that. I really did.

I finally broke out of the trees and into another large clearing. Cattle grazed here in surprising numbers. From what I could see, Bar X Bar was their brand to a one. I rode through them, scattering big-eyed playful calves and receiving doleful looks from their resentful mothers. The air smelled so fresh it hurt. The sky ahead of me was orange. I thought I would go just as far as I could before full dark.

The country grew a little more open, except along watercourses, which were heavily wooded. I came to one of these about dark — one containing a clear-watered little stream where walnut and hackberry trees grew and wild persimmons sprouted — where I decided to make camp for the night. It had rained very little there, and the ground was only mildly damp. I unsaddled my horse, let him drink, and tied him to a clump of bushes. Then I began trying to locate a good spot on which to bed down. Unless you have suffered a similar predicament, you can't imagine how miserable I was that night, trying to sleep in wet clothes with only a saddle for a pillow, no fire, and a half-wet saddle blanket for a cover. To this day, I remember how concerned I was that I would catch pneumonia or the gout because of it.

Dawn came, clear and cool. I awoke stiff and cold in every joint. I checked on my horse, then walked around a bit and stretched and walked some more. I wished not only that I had something to eat, but that I at least had prospects for obtaining something. I had no idea how far I would have to ride before coming upon someone who could help me out, but I decided that with steady riding surely I would accomplish that sometime during the day.

I saddled up and rode out, heading mostly west because I thought the nearest towns would lie in that direction. Too, I shouldn't have to cross a river to get to one—a fact not true of just about any other direction I might take.

I rode about an hour and saw mostly cows and grass and trees. I kept thinking I would stumble on some Bar X Bar riders, but I hadn't seen anyone at all so far.

Late morning found me approaching another tree-lined stream. I wasn't feeling too good—mostly, I figured, the combined result of too much sun on too empty a stomach after too poor a night's sleep. My thoughts turned to a good drink of water, shade, and maybe a short nap. I entered the trees without thinking to practice caution in my approach. That's probably the reason I rode smack dab into the middle of someone's camp without even realizing it was there until far too late to do anything to avoid it.

Three very familiar-looking horses nickered to my bay, and while my poor sun-dulled mind was still trying to put things it should have recognized immediately together, two men came lurching up from their bedrolls with guns drawn.

I stared stupidly at their unshaven, bleary-eyed visages as one of them said, "Well, I'll be damned. T.G., what the hell are you doing here?"

I sighed and slumped in my saddle. It was Kansas and Buster, caught sleeping off a good drunk they had enjoyed the night before at Pawnee. They informed me of this only after I somewhat resignedly told them all about my having got "lost" from Clyde the day before back near the hideout.

They sure did have a good laugh over it, let me te

CHAPTER 12

WE arrived back at the Triangle camp an hour past dark. You would think that Clyde, presented with a packhorse loaded with grub and supplies, two somewhat overdue gang members, and one errant captive thought forever lost, would have at least been happy to see us. If he was, he sure seemed determined not to show it—especially in my case.

"I spent my whole day looking for you, T.G.—my whole damned day!"

"You ran off and left me," I told him. "I got lost in the rain; I had no idea where you went."

He gave me an accusatory look. "You just kept right on riding, is what you did."

I shrugged. "What did you expect me to do? Hang around so I could be caught again? Do you think me a fool?"

"He's right, Clyde," Kansas said. "It was your fault all the way. No use being mad at him."

Clyde's mood was not improved. "I'm not going to be very trusting from now on, T.G. You realize that, don't you?"

"I won't be expecting you to," I said stiffly.

We were all standing in front of the cabin, a notably quiet Janie and Juice hovering in the background and our horses still awaiting an unsaddling nearby.

"Let's stop all this jawing." Buster said. "We've still got a pack to unload and horses to tend to, and I'm starving. What about it, Janie? Can you have us something to eat by the time we're back from the corrals?"

Not much was said as we unsaddled our horses. I helped Buster with the pack while Kansas and Clyde led the horses on over to the corrals. Inside the cabin, Juice hobbled around trying to help Janie. By the time Buster and I had deposited saddles and gear and put up the supplies, Clyde and Kansas were back.

Those of us who had come in late ate supper in dead silence, partly because we were too hungry to talk but mostly because the tension of earlier had not subsided. When we were finished with this and the dishes, Janie announced that she was tired and was going to bed; the rest of us could stay up and stare at one another all we wanted.

Ten minutes later, when we were all either in bed or nearly there, Clyde went over to douse the lantern.

I heard him pulling his bunk over by the door in the dark, and when I thought he was in bed, I said, "I still haven't found out, Clyde—did you catch the horse?"

"The horse? What horse?"

"Why, Juice's horse. Yesterday, in the rain. Did you catch it?"

For a moment there was dead silence. "Yeah—I caught the horse."

"Well, I guess that much is good anyway."

"Go to sleep, T.G."

He never said another word on the subject of my attempted escape from the Triangle camp.

Kansas had another newspaper, one he had picked up in Pawnee but was actually a Stillwater paper. It was over two weeks old and did not contain anything about the gang's robbery of my Katy train near Wagoner. But it did have an editorial on the Daltons, a rather fiery tirade against them and the law officers who were supposed to be hunting them down. I couldn't believe the way Clyde pored over and over that article. It was the one subject that never tired him, I guess.

We were all sitting around the table after supper the next night— everyone but Janie, who had just left to go for her nightly sponge bath near the spring. Clyde had been reading some of the choice parts to us.

"You know, you shouldn't be so single-minded, Clyde," Kansas remarked when the reading seemed finished. "It keeps you from being a well-rounded individual, is what it does."

Clyde ignored this. "Tell me again what you heard in Pawnee about that little escapade Juice and I pulled off south of the Cimarron."

Kansas sighed. "You tell him, Buster. I'm tired of talking about it. Maybe you can add something I forgot."

Buster wagged his head wearily. "Dammit, Clyde, what more is there to tell? Two fellows in the saloon told us all about how they were in that little town when the general store and post office were robbed and a good horse was stolen from the local livery. They told us that a few figured it was some of the Dalton gang that did it; others argued it couldn't have been, that the Dalton boys would never sink so low, that they are good boys who wouldn't do the little man any harm—just the railroads and such. Others say those boys were horse thieves before they were train robbers. The only reason they haven't sunk any lower is because they haven't thought of what that might be yet."

"And the posses? They looked for us for a week after we gave them the slip the second time and gave up."

"That's what those two fellows said."

"They thought we had headed for the Osage Hills country?"

"Seems that way."

Clyde nodded in a self-satisfied way. "Good. Real good."

"So what's next, Clyde?" Buster wanted to know. "We've hung around here till we're ready to chew rocks. When do we do a really big job?"

"He can't tell you that with me here," I said.

Buster gave me a look. "And why in hell not? You ain't going nowhere."

I didn't say a thing to this. I didn't figure it was safe.

"The messenger's right," Clyde said. "I'll tell you when I'm ready."

"And when, approximately, will that be?"

"Not long," he promised. "Not long at all."

Somebody suggested we take our chairs outside where there was a breeze. It was muggy outside too, but not close, as it was in the cabin. There wasn't much of a breeze, though, and there were mosquitos. Kansas rolled a cigarette and began blowing smoke at them.

"Tell us, T.G.," he said conversationally, "when will your next escape attempt come? You've tried twice now and failed both times. Have you any new plans?"

"Neither of those times were really planned," I said. "They just sort of came about and I couldn't help myself."

He considered this. "I see. Well, do you think next time you might think it out ahead of time?"

I stared thoughtfully at the fire on the end of his cigarette. "There may not be a next time, Kansas. Those other occasions were just so discouraging I don't know if I can go through it again."

A moment of silence indicated that Kansas had not gotten the answer he had anticipated. "Okay, what are your plans then, T.G.? Assuming you had a choice, of course."

I pretended to think about it, *did* think about it. "Well, maybe I'll just become an outlaw. I know this gang I might apply for membership in. Maybe I'll just do that."

A heretofore silent Clyde said, "Very funny, T.G."

"Why?" I said. "What if I was serious? What would you say?"

"I would say you're crazy."

"You're an outlaw. Are you saying I would be crazy to want to be one too?"

"I'm saying you'd be crazy to think we'd believe you, that's what I'm saying."

Suddenly I found myself squaring to face him in dead earnest, which surprised even me.

"How could I prove it to you? Just say I was serious. How could I ever convince you I wanted to be a member of your gang?"

For just an instant he actually seemed to consider it.

"That's pretty theoretical, T.G. Given the circumstances here, I'm not sure you ever could."

"Think about it, though," I insisted. "Come up with something. Just see if I'm not game."

"Well, I'll be damned," Kansas finally said. "I don't think I believe this."

I guess they all felt about that way, for there sure was a load of thoughtful silence just then. No telling what would have broken it, had Janie not suddenly come charging in among us, out of breath, as if she had run all the way back from the spring.

"Damn your . . . hides . . . Have any of you . . . been gone from here . . . while I was at the spring?" She stood in the light of the doorway, looking disheveled and maybe a bit frightened. She had gone for her bath unarmed.

Buster seemed about to say something funny, but Clyde stopped him. "What is it? Why'd you ask that?"

"Just tell me more,"she insisted. "Did anyone leave here while I was gone?"

Clyde rose and looked around at the rest of us, as if trying to recall for certain. "No. No, I don't think anyone did. We've all been here right along."

"Then I think we have a problem," she said. "I'm sure I heard someone skulking around in the brush near the spring a few minutes ago. I heard him curse when he must have stumbled on something. I ran almost all the way here, even though I thought it might only have been one of you playing tricks."

Clyde just stared at her.

"I think he watched me while I bathed," she said.

A moon, far from full but very bright, hung in the sky to the west of us. Out away from the light of the cabin, things did not seem terribly dark at all. I was crouched in tall grass about fifty yards in back of the cabin, near the creek. Three or four feet away was Janie, armed now with both six-gun and rifle.

We were alone there, left to watch the cabin while Clyde, Buster, and Kansas had slipped away in the darkness to see if they could locate the intruder. Juice was stationed in front of the cabin, also beyond the light cast by the lantern left burning in the main room. It had all been done very quietly, the gang leaving the cabin one or two at a time so as not to arouse the suspicions of anyone watching.

I was assigned to stay with Janie, partly to keep me out of the way and of course to make sure that someone kept an eye on me.

"I don't doubt that you heard something, Janie," I told her in a low voice. "But who on earth would be snooping around way out here?"

"Don't ask me," she said. "But I know someone was there. I heard a noise in the brush and then that curse. I might have passed it off as some kind of animal but for the voice. It was a man's voice, I'd swear to that."

"Could there have been more than one person?"

"There could have been twenty. I only heard one."

For a while we just sat there. The creek trickled lightly ahead of us. One of the horses cleared its nostrils from the corrals. A slight breeze caused the grass to wave. A tree somewhere was full of noisy cicadas.

"I can't see anything, can you?" Janie asked presently.

"Just moonlight and shadows," I said.

"Maybe we won't find him now. Maybe he got away."

"That's possible. He probably knew you'd heard him the minute you ran away."

"I didn't exactly run right away," she said. "I finished dressing as if I never heard him. I didn't run till I was pretty sure I was beyond his view."

I searched what I could see of our surroundings for signs of life. The cicadas only seemed to grow more noisy, the shadows deeper. Janie grew impatient.

"Why haven't we heard something from Clyde and the others by now? How long has it been?"

I shrugged. "Twenty minutes, maybe half an hour. Don't get excited. Like you said, we may not find him now. And if we don't, it will take a while to make sure; if he's still around, we'll know soon enough."

I didn't think of myself as prophetic then, and I don't now, but sometimes what a person just idly predicts turns out to make him look that way. Sometimes he would just as soon have been wrong.

A noise in the grass across the creek from us caused both of us to straighten. It could have been almost anything—an animal large or small, a man . . . Janie gripped my left arm with one hand, but neither of us said anything. Whatever it was, it had sounded far too close by for us to risk even a whisper. We just stared into the darkness, wishing the moon were brighter and straining both ears and eyes trying to detect what had made the noise.

We heard it again, only a little downstream from us this time. It was a rustling in the grass, something moving away from us. Janie released my arm and hefted her rifle to a ready position. Something moved in some brush farther downstream and we thought we heard low voices. Our eyes locked in mutual alarm. We had no way of knowing who was who, if Clyde, Buster, and Kansas were nearby, or if Janie's peeping Tom had friends.

For a few moments nothing at all happened. Then the cicadas stopped, so suddenly it was as if all the world had magically turned silent. We almost hesitated to breathe, and I would have sworn I could hear both of our hearts thumping.

There was another noise in the grass, only this time from upstream. From the brush downstream, we heard a loud whisper.

"That's Kansas. He's above him now!" It sounded like Buster. A not quite so loud "Sssssh!" sounded very much like Clyde.

And then all hell broke loose. Something splashed in the creek and came crashing through the tall grass in our direction. Someone yelled, "Stop, damn you, or I'll shoot!"

A form appeared coming right at Janie and me. A shot blasted from across the creek, and I saw the muzzle flash just before the dark figure lurched into me. I tried to avoid him, but I wasn't quick enough. Janie screamed as the figure and I collapsed in a heap.

He wasn't very strong, but he sure was desperate. He scrambled wildly, trying to regain his feet. I grabbed one leg and held on for dear life, while Janie screamed, "Don't shoot! Don't anybody else shoot! We've got him over here!"

I had him all right—by one ankle, just barely. He was kicking like a three-month-old calf about to be flanked and thrown. He fell once but struggled right back up, and I suppose he would have kicked and beat me over the head until I was forced to let go if Janie hadn't finally thought to stick the muzzle of her rifle in his ribs.

"I'll blow a hole in you the size a wagon could go through if you don't stop!" she told him, thumbing back the hammer. "Believe me, I will!"

Clyde, Buster, and Kansas all arrived at once, charging through the grass like thrashing machines, huffing and puffing and yelling at one another to "hurry up" and "hold your fire" and "where in hell is anybody, anyway?"

A few minutes later, we had dragged our prisoner over to the cabin, where we were joined by Juice. We stood the man in the lantern light to get a good look at him. He was an old codger, gray-haired and rail-thin. His clothes were dirty and his pants were held up by suspenders. Apparently he got his own first good look at us as well; he seemed disappointed.

"Who are you people, anyway?" he asked. "For a while there, I thought sure you was the Dalton gang. But I know all them boys, know 'em well. And that sure as hell ain't who any of *you* are!"

CHAPTER 13

WE marched the old man inside and sat him down at the table, around which the Crosby gang gathered with serious interrogation on their minds.

Clyde, of course, was the gang's spokesman. "What made you think we might be the Dalton gang? What were you doing here in the first place?"

The old man had the clearest of blue eyes. His face was tanned as dark as brown-polished shoe leather and had at least a thousand wrinkles. He was missing most of his front teeth, and the ones he had left were long and yellow, like those of an old horse. From the gray bristles on his face, I judged he must not have shaved in a week.

"There's a posse in these parts, on the scout for the Dalton boys," he said in a shrill voice. "I come to warn 'em, is all."

"You came to *what?*"

"You heard me," the old man said, his eyes darting here and there. "Them boys has got friends in this territory, lots of 'em. This posse hired me on as a guide to lead 'em into the Triangle. I snuck away early this mornin', thinkin' to see if I could find the boys, and let 'em know what's up. They wouldn't have a chance with that posse, let me tell you. Twenty-five good men, all armed to the teeth and led by a couple of deputy U.S. marshals. Not a chance, by damn, unless they was warned aforehand."

Clyde asked with narrowed eyes, "What's in it for you if you warn these fellows? Especially when a posse's paying you to help find them. Why tell us?"

"Them boys done me a favor once. They're good at that, doin' poor folks like me favors. They know folks don't forget. I sort of figured you folks might understand how that is."

Clyde remained skeptical. "How did you get here? Where's your horse? And why sneak around when you could just come on up to the house and introduce yourself?"

The old man never batted an eye. "Ain't got no horse. Got a mare mule. She's tied to a tree beyond that runty little creek you got back yonder. And I was sneakin' around, as you call it, because I first wanted to make sure who you was. I was circlin' around, tryin' to stay with the trees, when I run up on someone a-bathin' up at that spring up there. Everything just got outa hand after that."

"I'll say it did," Clyde agreed. "That was my sister you spied on at the spring."

The old man squinted at Janie as if he hadn't even noticed her since she had stuck her rifle in his ribs. "Your sister, huh? Yeah, well, if you say so."

"Take my word for it, old man," Clyde said icily. "Did you think *her* one of the Daltons? A woman?"

He shrugged. "Could've been. I hear tell Bob Dalton's got a galfriend who is sometimes seen with the gang. Some think she's Daisy Bryant, sister to Blackface Charley; others give her the name Eugenia Moore. She ain't as pretty as this 'un, though. Even without seein' her, I can just about swear to that."

"Maybe you just didn't see as *much* of her as you did of me," Janie retorted stiffly. "It doesn't say a lot for you, you know—being a peeper and all."

This old man didn't seem ready to back down from anything. "Look, young lady, I'm too old and have seen too much to be peepin' on anybody. I come onto you unknowin'-like and didn't see enough to excite even one of these young scoundrels. I tripped and dang near broke my neck, is what I did. When I looked up, you was gone. I went over to the spring, got me a drink, and was headed back for my mule when I figured out someone was stalkin' me. Wasn't long after that when you folks surrounded me and started shootin' and stuff. That's all there is to it."

"Tell us about the posse," Clyde said. "What makes them think the Daltons are around here?"

"They think that," the old man said, "'cause 'here' is where outlaws go to hide. And 'cause they haven't been able to find 'em anyplace else. They've been like ghosts ever since that Red Rock train robbery, the first of June."

Clyde's eyes narrowed, somewhat in surprise. "Red Rock? Was that their last job?"

"Well," the old man said with some deliberation, "folks can hardly tell for sure. There's been all kinds of stuff blamed on 'em. Take that train holdup near Wagoner two weeks after Red Rock. A couple of the robbers, it's said, actually called each other by the names of Bob and Emmett right there for everyone to hear. Some say they was fakes and that the deal was spoiled by the express messenger who claimed to know Bob and Emmett and spoke up right in front of the robbers that he knew they wasn't them. And you know what? Them robbers took the messenger with 'em and nary a thing's been seen of him since. Some say it really was the Daltons and the messenger was in on it with 'em. I guess no one really knows for sure, except ain't it strange that messenger's never been heard from again?" It was then and only then that I caught the old man's eyes on me, and I became very uncomfortable because of it.

"They probably killed him," Kansas offered innocently.

"Mebbeso," the old man said with an indifferent shrug.

I had sat somewhat mesmerized throughout this discussion, and I suddenly felt Clyde's eyes on me. I met his gaze and very slowly wagged my head to indicate that I had no intention of saying a word.

The old man said, "A posse almost had what was thought to be that same bunch over in the Creek Nation shortly after the holdup. They showed up and camped on a half-blood's place and the half-blood turned 'em in. Said he knew their leader, but not by name. He didn't know if they was Daltons or not and wouldn't say where he'd met the leader. Needless to say, they slipped the posse and so far as I know ain't been seen since."

It was impossible to tell what Clyde's reaction to all of this was. He just sat there looking amazed.

The old man said, "You folks, now . . . who are you? I ain't talkin' to just such a gang of outlaws, am I?"

Clyde smiled. "You should've thought of that before you did all that talking, seems to me."

The old man just stared at him.

Clyde laughed. "Hey, don't worry. This is a cow camp, nothing more. We're Bar X Bar and have nothing to do with outlaws, except now and then some strangers take a meal with us, no questions asked. All we know is cows and horses, that's it."

The old man's eyes were on Janie. "A woman in a cow camp? You expect me to believe *that?*"

Clyde stiffened. "She's my sister, old fella. Remember, I told you that? She's our cook here, no more, no less. She can ride with the men if she has to, but that's all she does with them. Do you get my drift?"

I guess the old man thought it good policy to say that he did. "Well, yeah. And say, if she's a cook, I don't suppose a feeble old man who hasn't had food since yesterday could get a bite to eat around here, now could he?"

That old man who so appreciated favors was fed and allowed to spend the night with us without ever knowing that he was under guard the entire time. The next morning he was fed again before being sent on his way.

His mule was located and brought in by Kansas and Buster shortly after breakfast.

"Just tell that posse the Daltons haven't been seen anywhere around here," Clyde told him as he mounted up. "Tell them they might as well spend their time someplace else."

"I think I'll do that," the old man promised. "I just sure as hell think I will."

Kansas watched him pass beyond earshot, then asked, "Do you reckon he really believed that stuff about us being cowhands?"

"Hardly a chance of it," Clyde replied. "But it doesn't matter. We won't be here long, anyway. We're pulling out. With a posse in the area it's not smart for us to stay on here. I know a place farther west, on the North Canadian River, that'll do just as well."

Kansas stared at him. "Are you serious?"

He nodded. "I thought all night on it. We'll divide up and go in two groups. I'll draw a map for the group that's not with me. Come on, the sooner we're gone the better."

For the most part, we just stood and gawked at him.

"Well, did you hear me or didn't you?"

Clyde picked Janie and me to go with him. Apparently he was determined to keep a personal eye on both of us. In Janie's case, of course, he was just being a protective big brother. In mine, well, if I tried to get away again, I suppose he intended to be the first one there to stop me.

He spent a full fifteen minutes describing to Kansas, Buster, and Juice how to reach the rendezvous on the North Canadian. The only map he drew was in the dust in front of the cabin, and that was later scratched out. Janie and I looked on and figured we could have made it there blindfolded ourselves.

"You've learned a lot about this country in a year, Clyde," I told him. "You must have traveled far and wide finding hideouts like that."

"That's very observant of you, T.G. Very observant."

We packed our gear in a deceptively unhurried but efficient manner. I compared it to what I imagined might be a tribe of Plains Indians breaking camp to move on in the face of an approaching enemy. The plan was that we should meet on the North Canadian in about a week.

"My group will take the packhorse," Clyde told Kansas, Buster, and Juice. "You're welcome to all the provisions you can carry on your saddles. It's up to you if you want to acquire more—and another packhorse—along the way. Just don't do anything stupid while you're about it, okay?"

We all rode out together at ten o'clock that morning. About halfway down the clearing, we split up. Kansas, Buster, and Juice peeled off to the left and entered the trees, where they quickly disappeared. Clyde, Janie, and I pulled up just short of the woods at the far end of the clearing and looked back toward the cabin. It was out of our view now, but we could see about where it lay.

"I liked it there," Janie said. "I'm not sure I really want to leave."

"You'll get over it soon enough," Clyde told her. "You'll like things just as well where we're going."

She stared at him. "What makes you think that? I thought you told me once that was short-grass country, all open and treeless and not very pretty at all."

"A lot of it is. But some places are better than others. And there are always trees of some sort along the stream bottoms. You'll see."

We rode on, fully unaware until much later that a posse of twenty-five men had just descended on the cabin behind us and would soon be working hard to figure out our trail.

We entered a more open country to the south and west. We saw cattle but no people. About one o'clock we came to a tree-lined stream that looked very familiar to me. We stopped to eat the lunch Janie had packed for us, and finally it came to me.

"I camped here the night I got away! I'd swear it was right here, this very place under these hackberry trees!"

Clyde was tying his horse and the packhorse to a bush. "Fond memory, eh, T.G.?"

"It could have been fonder," I said.

Janie came around with some cold biscuits and cold fried quail that had been left over from breakfast, and we sat down on the creek bank to eat.

"I'm sure it was right here," I said again. "Isn't that something?"

Clyde didn't seem impressed. "We're following a well-used trail, probably the same one you stumbled on. It's not surprising we've wound up at the same creek crossing."

A thought seemed to occur to Janie then. "Do you suppose that's wise, Clyde? For us to use a well-traveled trail? What if someone is following us?"

Clyde frowned. "Following us? Now, who in hell would be doing a think like that?"

Nonetheless, I noticed that once the creek was forded we no longer followed a well-traveled trail. We also angled more and more southward, the Cimarron and the Sac and Fox or Iowa reservations in mind.

"We'll lose ourselves in the Cross Timbers," Clyde told us. "Later we'll turn back west toward short-grass country." The Cross Timbers was that narrow tangle of woods that ran north and south across the central part of what is now Oklahoma. It qualified as one of the best places ever in which to lose oneself.

Just past sundown another watercourse came into view, at least a mile away. We were full in the open, the nearest trees ahead being those that lined the watercourse. A half mile away a low hill covered with blackjacks marked our back trail. I don't know why I happened to look back there, but I did, just in time to see a group of riders emerge from the trees at the base of that little hill.

"Clyde," I said. He was riding only slightly ahead of me and off to one side. "Look back there."

The riders must have spotted us even before they reached the base of the hill, for they were coming at a pretty good clip. They were at least a dozen in number, and even on our worst days we would not have mistaken them for a bunch of Bar X Bar cowhands out for a Sunday ride.

Clyde didn't waste a minute. "Head for the creek bottom and the trees!"

We plunged forward, Janie in the lead, me in the middle, and Clyde bringing up the rear with the packhorse. Our horses must have been fresher than theirs, for we were outdistancing them handsomely when we reached the first of the trees. We pulled up to take a look back. They were coming in a dust cloud, and as we struggled to control our excited mounts, the first shots were fired.

Clyde yelled, "The creek! There has to be a creek here somewhere. Ride down the creek!"

At first thick brush and trees seemed to bar our way. But with Clyde back there to drive us on, we knew there was only one way to go and that was straight ahead. We crashed through a thicket of shrubby stuff and were confronted with a small bluff that dropped steeply down toward a lazy little stream running about two feet deep and ten feet wide. The bluff itself was about eight feet in height.

Janie's horse, and then mine, took the bluff almost without pause and went sliding on their haunches into the creek. Clyde's mount and the packhorse were right on our heels.

"Stay in the water," Clyde told us. "Don't leave the water."

We splashed and clattered down the stream bed, once again with Janie in the lead and Clyde bringing up the rear. Soon the banks on both sides of us became less abrupt, and a broadening bottomland became evident beneath the trees.

Behind us we heard yells and shouts; our pursuers had gained appreciably on us and were now not far behind us at all.

"Oh, hell!" Clyde said. The light was growing poor and we couldn't see them yet, but that was mostly because of the winding vagaries of the stream bed. We splashed onward in a poorly organized rush. I was beginning to wonder if there was any way we could avoid being overtaken.

And then, as we rounded a bend in the creek, we surprised a bunch of cows that had come down to the water for a drink. A couple of them were standing in the middle of the stream; others were lined up along the bank, and apparently still others were trailing in through the brush behind these.

"Whoa up!" Clyde hollered.

At first the cattle seemed so startled they didn't react. But then those on the bank whirled to run. The two in the water lunged to follow suit.

Clyde yelled, "Go with them! Ride in among them!"

Janie hesitated. "What? Do *what*?"

"Just do as I say, dammit—go!"

We went. Janie, then me, then Clyde, scrambling madly up the bank after the cows. The brush was thick along the bank but thinned out considerably away from it. Cattle were everywhere. We charged in among them, mostly only scattering them further, but managing to outdistance a few in such a way that our tracks were laid ahead of theirs and hopefully trampled out by them.

We had crossed about two hundred yards of generally open area when Clyde called ahead for us to turn toward a thick tangle of trees and brush.

"In there, quick!"

We pulled up within the trees to look back the way we had come. Even in the poor light, we could see that many of the cattle we had scattered had taken to the brush just as we had; some, on the other hand, had remained in the open, and several already seemed headed back to water. These weren't destined to get far, however, as once again riders burst among them, coming out of the brush that lined the stream. Cows again went in all directions, causing Clyde to curse. "Dammit, who in hell are those guys?"

Janie looked at him. "Why, it has to be that posse that old man told us about. Who else could it be?"

Clyde seemed unsure. "I only count a dozen or so of them. The old man said twenty-five."

"Maybe they split up," I suggested. "Maybe some of them went after Kansas, Buster, and Juice."

Clyde nodded thoughtfully. "Yeah, that's probably it, all right."

"So what are we going to do?" Janie asked nervously.

"Just hold on. We'll see what they do first. It's almost dark. Let's just give it a few minutes."

Janie said, "I think they are mostly confused. Look at them!"

They were milling about, looking at the ground.

Clyde almost smiled. "They can't find our tracks. Those cows did the trick on them, damned if they didn't!"

"Don't be too sure about that," I warned. "Look there—a couple of them are coming this way."

Janie looked at Clyde. "What do you think?"

"They're not tracking cows," he admitted glumly.

Sure enough, they kept right on coming, their eyes glued to the ground, until they reached a point at which one of them turned and waved to the balance of the posse.

"Damn," Clyde said in disgust.

We were looking around for a way to ease on out of there when Janie said, "Wait a minute. They're fanning out. Maybe it's not going to be so easy for them after all."

In the poor light, and with all the confusion in the tracks, it probably wasn't. But Clyde was in no mood to wait and see. He pointed Janie and me into the trees. A half moon was in the sky to the west, but in those dense woods just then, all was a maze of shadow mixed with early twilight and the moon was to be seen only through this and that brief break in the trees. Clyde hung back briefly, but then quickly caught up.

"They're still coming," he called ahead to us.

"Where do you want me to go, Clyde?" Janie called back from her place in the lead. "I can't tell a thing about what's ahead."

"Just keep going. Don't worry about it."

"But I don't like having to lead in this stuff. I'm afraid I'll get turned around and take us right back the way we've come."

I heard a disgusted sigh behind me. "Aw, hell. All right, pull up and come on back here. I'll lead."

They switched places, Clyde continuing to lead the packhorse. We tried to stay in line with the moon in order to remain headed generally west. I don't know how effective this was, as darkness rapidly overtook us and we couldn't even see the moon for the trees at times. Too, we were forced to wind our way around a lot because of the denseness of the woods.

As a result, we must have gotten turned around, for suddenly Clyde pulled up and whispered back to us, "Voices. I'd swear I heard voices up ahead."

I don't know about Janie, but I couldn't hear a thing. I couldn't see much, either. The moon was blotted out where we were and the woods were denser than ever. The next thing I knew, Clyde was dismounting and coming back to hand me his horse's reins and the packhorse's lead rope.

"I know I heard voices up there," he whispered. "You two stay here and keep an eye on the horses. I'm gonna sneak up there on foot and see if I can see who it is."

Janie and I watched the night shadows envelope him, then exchanged glances. Because we were in heavy shadow, we could just make out one another's features even though we were no more than five feet apart.

"This is spooky, T.G.," Janie said. "I wish Clyde hadn't gone off like that."

"I just hope he can find his way back," I replied seriously.

For several minutes we just sat there, listening to the routine voices of the night. And then we heard something that definitely was not routine. Voices . . . someone moving through the trees, the clink of a spur, the rattle of a bit chain. They couldn't have been more than twenty-five yards away. I held my breath. The voices, though kept low, became distinct.

"Hey, Carl, you see anything yet?"

"Naw, nothing, Seth. You?"

"No, and I don't like this one bit. What if they *are* in here? How in hell are we gonna see them before they see us? What's to keep someone from blowing us right out of the saddle before we know they're even around?"

"I dunno. Maybe if we don't talk so much, they at least won't hear us."

This didn't seem to have much effect on Seth. "Hear us? Hell, twelve mounted men in woods like these, and we're supposed to keep from being heard?"

They were almost upon us, and my most immediate fear was that one of our horses would nicker and give us away.

"If you ask me, we're all crazy to come in here after dark this way, Seth went on. "We shoulda just made camp and waited till morning."

"I know, I know," Carl replied. "But you know Bill. When he's determined, he's determined."

They were passing to my right when suddenly a voice came from somewhere to our left. "Hey, you guys, shut up over there! You think these people we're after are deaf?"

I heard a soft curse from my right but nothing else was said. I could hear them in the brush, past me now but still close enough that I could very easily call out to them. Without a doubt, it there ever was going to be a perfect opportunity for me to be rescued, it was at hand. There would be almost nothing Janie could do about it and probably no way Clyde—wherever he was—could interfere. I could call to those men and in minutes it would be all over.

But I didn't do it. I simply sat there quietly and let them pass by, half expecting our horses to give us away and somehow glad when it turned out that none of them did. Pretty soon we could no longer hear any of the posse moving about.

Finally Janie whispered. "Do you think they're gone, T.G.?"

"Yes, I think so."

"You know, I couldn't have stopped you if you had called to them."

"I know."

"But still you didn't."

"No."

A noise in the brush started us, followed by a whispered, "Hold your hardware! It's me—Clyde!"

He appeared only a few feet from my horse, which was spooked enough already and almost shied from under me.

"Did you hear them, Clyde?" Janie asked. "Did you see them? T.G. could have reached out and touched a couple of them. He could have given us away easily. He just let them go."

"Yeah, I know." He took his reins and mounted his horse. "That was decent of you, T.G. I wasn't fifty feet away when those fellows rode past. Why'd you do it?"

I shrugged. "I keep asking myself things like that."

He was silent for a few moments before saying, "Well, we can't hang around just jawing like this. We've got to get out of here before some of the rest of that posse stumbles onto us. I figure we'll double back on them and be long gone by the time daylight comes."

He took the packhorse's lead rope and reined around. Janie rode briefly up beside me as we started out. I almost couldn't make her out, there in the shadows.

"I don't know why you did it either, T.G. But thank you; thank you once again."

I tried to make light of it. "It wasn't so much. Besides, those guys were hunting the Daltons. What would they know or even care about me?"

We slipped on out of there undetected without me even suspecting how wrong I was about this. As I was to learn later, that posse wasn't just looking for the Daltons; that old man we had caught and let go (Clyde was a fool for doing that) had been blowing smoke all over the place when he had said that they were; he was a spy for the posse, was all. As much as anything else, they were on the lookout for me. He knew that but had been unable to identify me for certain —partly because he never heard any member of the gang call me by name—while he was with us. He had not fallen for the bit about us being cowhands, though, and it was on that note that he had put the posse onto us.

But even this information wasn't the real stunner for me, when I finally learned the truth of it all. Riding as a member of that posse we so easily went off and left stumbling around in those darkened woods was my own brother Sam—come all the way from Missouri hoping to help find me.

CHAPTER 14

IT took us eight days to reach the rendezvous on the North Canadian. It shouldn't have taken that long; in straight-line distance we wound up little more than a hundred and fifty miles from our starting point in the Triangle. But we didn't travel in a straight line. For the first four days we traveled only at night, and part of that on done-in horses. On more than one occasion we traveled miles out of our way just to avoid a town or a settled farming area. We had to be very careful selecting places to hole up during the day.

On the third day, I figure somewhere in Kickapoo country, we snuck into an Indian's horse pasture and stole fresh mounts, abandoning our own. I actually hated to part with my bay, but like the others he was pretty well worn out. We even acquired a fresh packhorse. The Indian horses were not as good as our old ones, but they were fresh and wiry and the best we could do at the time.

We went generally south following our narrow brush with the posse in the Triangle country, and after crossing the Cimarron River that same night. Much of our trek was in the Cross Timbers, and I decided during that episode that if I never saw another blackjack or shinnery or briar I would be just that much happier.

We came upon and crossed the North Canadian that same night, still over a hundred miles downstream from our destination.

We worked our way south of Oklahoma City the next evening, then holed up before midnight. The next morning Clyde, for the first time, had us on the move in broad daylight. He claimed he didn't know the country thereabouts well enough to travel at night anymore. Besides, there had been no sign of further pursuit by the posse.

We avoided populated areas as best we could, however, until late that afternoon Clyde did something that neither Janie nor I could quite get him to satisfactorily explain. We came to and rode straight down the middle of a small town of El Reno, located but a short distance from the south bank of the North Canadian at the junction of the Choctaw and Rock Island railroads. Across the river was the recently abandoned site of Reno City, left that way upon being spurned by the railroads in favor of the El Reno location.

We came to a general store, stopped briefly and bought a number of supplies, and then rode on. The only thing I remember otherwise was that Clyde kept eyeing things as if he were mentally cataloguing their locations for later reference. I didn't notice at the time that key among these was the town's leading bank.Also, it occurred to me only vaguely how trusting Clyde was being to let me ride into a town like that. I could have given him and Janie away any time I wanted to.

A few miles beyond El Reno, we passed within sight of Fort Reno, established in the 1870s to protect the Darlington Indian Agency from Cheyenne raids. This we did take pains to avoid as we angled northwest, following the slant of the river valley.

Over the next three days, we passed through sections of newly opened Arapaho country, swung well south of the military post, Cantonment, entered the Cherokee Strip, and crossed the Deep Creek bottoms near where that stream meets the North Canadian and where the Deep Creek cattle trail made its crossing of the river. From there we crossed Bent Creek, then Persimmon Creek, and finally drew within sight of a certain bend in the river that Clyde said was the one we were looking for.

We found our crossing and, across the river, in a certain copse of trees, we came upon the simple dugout with a sod roof and no sign of recent occupancy that was to be our place of rendezvous with the rest of the gang.

We were little surprised that the other three gang members had failed to arrive ahead of us. Knowing what we had gone through to get there ourselves, we could easily imagine someone taking even longer. After all, most of the country behind us had now been opened to white settlement—the Unassigned Lands in that first big run of 1889, the Cheyenne and Arapaho lands in April of 1892— and people were everywhere in what had once been a wilderness with only a few Indians and even fewer white cattlemen and cowboys to interfere with one's comings and goings. We figured that Kansas, Buster, and Juice might arrive as much as two days after us with nothing unusual about it.

Clyde didn't seem to be much bothered about this, but there were a few things that displeased him immensely about the condition of that fine hideout he had so bragged about eight days before.

First, we weren't long in finding that the dugout had become infested with rattlesnakes and was thus unfit for human habitation. We had been looking forward to having a roof over our heads again, but not under those circumstances. Not only would we continue to sleep on the ground for the foreseeable future, we would do it well away from the dugout.

Too, a small creek ran to the river through that copse of trees — mostly tall cottonwoods. When Clyde had visited the site before, the creek had flowed clear water within twenty yards of the dugout. Now it was bone dry, and if we were to have water it must be river water of lesser quality.

Worst of all, perhaps, was what we had learned from a group of cowboys guarding a large herd of cattle on the Deep Creek Trail a day earlier. Not only had the lands to the south and southeast of us been opened for settlement, but the Cherokee Strip was destined for the same fate. For over a year, the U.S. government had been attempting to rid the Strip of the cattlemen who were using those lands for grazing. Troops from nearby Fort Supply and elsewhere were all over the place, looking to evict "trespass" cattle — not to mention their owners and handlers — from the area.

So far, the cattlemen were cooperating poorly. Some of them, the minute escorting troops had taken them across one or the other of the Strip's boundaries and turned to ride away, immediately made plans to turn their herds around and reenter the off-limits lands. After all, the Cherokee Strip Livestock Association had signed a ten-year agreement for grazing rights with the Cherokees and some of the cattlemen had ranched in the Strip for years. They figured they had their rights, while the government stubbornly figured otherwise. The worst of the problems seemed to be occurring to the north and east of us, south of Kiowa, Kansas and along the cedar breaks of the Cimarron. Clyde was not happy with the developments, in any event.

"That's all we need," he lamented as we finished staking our horses out to graze and turned to arranging our camp. "Army troopers riding around poking their noses in things. Makes for a hell of a hideout!"

I was gazing out across what I could see of the treeless prairie of grama and buffalo grass, almost noe of which was over eight inches tall, and found myself unsure how good a hideout this could ever have been, anyway. I guess the area was isolated enough and probably always would be sparsely settled, even if the Strip was eventually to be opened. Outside the trees of the river bottom, however, there sure was a shortage of things to hide behind.

That evening, after supper, Janie and I strolled down to the river while Clyde sat lost in thought before our small campfire. Only the faintest signs of daylight were left in the sky, and gnats swarmed around us.

"Clyde sure is in a crummy mood tonight," I remarked as we walked.

Janie nodded. "He gets that way when he's trying to decide something."

"What's he trying to decide?"

"I don't know. I never do until he tells me later."

At the riverbank, we looked for, and found, a place to sit down. I leaned back. Full darkness had long since claimed our surroundings, but on the horizon to our left and a little behind us, the great creamy face of a waning full moon was just beginning to show itself. I couldn't help being reminded of another night much like it, back in Osage country, on a small tributary to the Arkansas River, Janie on one bank and me on the other. . . .

Janie seemed absorbed in watching the moon's growing reflection on the water. Suddenly she turned to me. "T.G., let's do something. A swim—it's been so long since I went for a swim!"

I just stared at her.

"Oh, I know," she said, her enthusiasm instantly dampened. "We can't go in together, at least not unless we wear our clothes."

"I don't think that would be much fun, all right," I agreed lamely.

"Well . . . maybe we could just go wading. The river is too shallow for swimming in most places anyway. Wading would at least cool us off and would be something fun to do. What do you think?"

"Well, I don't know," I said, really wanting to say yes but not at all sure it was a good idea. "This river has a lot of quicksand . . ."

"Oh, come on, T.G. It wasn't bad at all where we crossed it this afternoon. And besides, what's a little quicksand? You won't sink past your knees in it most times anyway. Come on, don't be such a worry wart. Let's be carefree just this once. Say yes, will you?"

Finally I relented. "Well, at least let's go back to the crossing. We know it's shallow there, and the bottom was pretty solid . . . It's right back that way, downstream."

She smiled as she got to her feet and offered me a hand up. "You're just too cautious, T.G. Do you know that? Too cautious sometimes even for your own good."

We followed the bank downstream till we reached the crossing. The bank sloped gently to the water's edge, as is the case with well-used fords.

We sat on the ground, took off our boots and socks and rolled up our pants legs to a point just above our knees.

"I feel like a ten-year-old kid," I mumbled.

"So feel that way. When you're old, you'll be wishing all the time that you could feel ten again."

"Now how in hell would you know that?"

She laughed. "I guess I don't. I just figure it that way, is all."

"Well, you're wrong," I said confidently. "When I'm old, I'll be wishing I was eighteen. That's what *I'll* be wishing."

The water was neither cold nor at first deep. About five yards out, however, it was already at our knees. I guess it only seemed more shallow than that when it was our horses doing the wading.

"Hmmmm." Janie considered. Being shorter than me, she was already in over her knees. She looked back with a somewhat sheepish grin.

"I don't know what to tell you," I said. "I don't think it will get much deeper, but it won't get much shallower, either."

"Shall we try to go all the way across?" It was almost a dare; I had no doubt that she intended to do just that.

"You're in the lead," I said.

She turned and took another step, very tentative. Soft mud oozed between my toes as I followed suit. The current swirled and felt good against my legs. We got about halfway across without going much deeper or sinking in quicksand, and once again Janie stopped.

"See, it's not so bad."

"We're not there yet," I said. "Just watch your step."

"Oh, don't worry, I will."

She soon wished she hadn't been so positive. I don't think she went three steps before she slipped, lost her balance, and with a little shriek went down with a splash. I was so startled I had no chance to do anything to prevent her fall. One moment she was standing up, the next she was flat on her back and flopping around. I bent to try to help her up, caught a thrashing hand, and before I knew it had lost my own balance and was hurtling head first into the water alongside of her. I came up spitting muddy water and looking all around. Janie was right there, sitting up with water to her armpits, trying to get both wet hair and water out of her eyes.

"Oh, T.G., I can't believe that happened! I just can't believe it!" She was somewhere between laughter and tears, maybe a little closer to the latter.

"I can," I grumped, sitting up also in a current that was not swift.

She gave a tentative smile. "You should see yourself."

"So should you," I retorted, not very good-naturedly.

She almost seemed to be fighting back laughter then. "We went swimming with our clothes on, after all, T.G."

I glared at her. "Oh, is *that* what we did?"

"Here, help me up," she said, extending both hands.

I struggled to my knees and took her hands—which was a mistake: I should have gotten all the way to my feet. I tried to rise as I was helping her, a counterbalancing act that did not work. Our hands slipped apart and we both fell back backward. We came up sputtering and flailing our arms and trying to keep from floating with the current. We wound up sitting there once again, facing one another and feeling completely ludicrous.

Finally I said, "Just stay where you are for a minute, okay?"

I rose, dripping, and once again extended my hands. She took them and this time came to her feet when I pulled. Still, her balance was questionable; she leaned instinctively against me to keep from falling, and I suddenly found myself with her in my arms. I couldn't help thrilling to the way her small, firm breasts felt against my chest through our wet shirts. And when I looked down, I discovered her face upraised within inches of mine. Her eyes were big, questioning, almost fearful, her lips slightly parted. I guess my eyes locked spontaneously, and with unmistakable intentions, on those lips.

"No, T.G.," she pleaded. "Please, no . . ."

But that was the only resistance she offered, and I guess there is no telling what might have led to what had a voice not interrupted us.

"Hey! What the hell do you two think you're doing out there? *Hey!*"

It was Clyde, standing on the riverbank, clearly visible in the bright moonlight and with hands on hips. He stood just that way, watching us, until we had sloshed our way back to dry land.

"I wouldn't even ask you to explain this," he told us, "except I sure do think it would be a good learning experience for us all if you'd make a stab at it."

We did such a fine job of it, he swore he'd never allow us out of his sight alone together again.

Three days later Kansas, Buster, and Juice finally showed up. By our best calculation, this was on the eighteenth of July. Clyde had worked himself into such a state of anxiety about them by then that he was almost ready to go looking for them. Naturally, his first words when the foursome came trooping into camp late that afternoon were a demand to know where they had been for so long.

Kansas shook his head wearily as he dismounted in front of us. "We've had a posse on our tails ever since we left the Triangle, Clyde. Half of one, at least. I figure it was part of the bunch that old man we caught told us about. I never saw anybody so damned determined. We've been all over trying to shake those jaspers—as far south as the Arbuckle Mountains, as far west as the Salt Fork of the Red. We've ridden down and stolen fresh horses twice since we last saw you, and it's only been the last three days that we haven't seen any sign of the posse and thought it safe to come here."

This really concerned Clyde, and it took quite a lot of talk by all three of them to convince him that they truly had shaken their pursuers.

Actually, they finally distracted him from it by telling him some news they had learned from some cowboys fording a herd of cattle on the South Canadian River a day earlier. It had to do with word just reaching that area about a daring holdup of Katy passenger train No. 2 at Adair, Indian Territory, on July 14. No less than eight robbers had been involved. T

CHAPTER 15

THE next night, past supper, Clyde had us gathered expectantly around the campfire. No one knew exactly what was about to transpire. Clyde had been thoughtful and uncommunicative all day. As Janie had said, he wasn't like that except when something was brewing.

He was the calmest I had seen him recently as he looked first at Juice and asked, "How's the foot? Any better today?" The little man had thrown away his crutch and could finally wear a boot, but he still hobbled around in obvious pain.

"'Bout the same, I reckon. Sore's healed, but something's wrong in the bones. I don't figure it'll ever get plumb well."

Clyde said, "Well, some progress is better than none, I guess. Anybody else got problems?"

Nobody volunteered any. We were as sound as four stout workhorses on good grain and fully conditioned to the plow.

"All right, good," he went on. "I have a plan for our next job. I think it's a good one, but I figure this thing has got to be done democratic. If you have suggestions, make them. I'll listen to you, just so long as you listen to me first."

"What about T.G.?" Buster wanted to know. "You including him in?"

Clyde never batted an eye. "He wants to be a member of the gang, remember? He told us, didn't he? Now's his chance to prove it."

I just gawked while Buster said, "You surprise me, Clyde."

"I told you what he did back in the Triangle," Clyde said. "He let the half of the posse that chased us go right on by when he could have called to them. Janie and I would most likely either be dead or standing in front of a federal judge right now, listening to our sentences, if he'd done anything but what he did."

He paused, waiting. Kansas, Buster, and Juice looked noncom-
mittal. Janie seemed ill at ease, but said nothing. I was as still as
stone.

Clyde nodded. "Okay, then. This deal will be a bank job. The
biggest haul we've ever made. Ten, maybe twenty thousand dollars.
It may not be easy, and it'll take more planning than anything
before, but it'll be worth it. I'm convinced of that."

He paused again to survey our reaction.

Kansas said, "Where, Clyde What bank?"

"El Reno. It's a little place, I know. But it's growing and it's at the
junction of two railroads. I think it'll be a good place to hit, and if we
work it right, a good one to get away from once we're done."

Buster looked uncertain. "Damn, I dunno. A bank. That'll have
to be in broad daylight, won't it?

"That's right. First thing in the morning, soon as the bank's open
for business and before any big withdrawals are made."

He leaned forward and picked up a small stick. He scratched lines
on the ground as he spoke. "This is the main street through town.
Right here is the bank. Over there is the jail and here is where they
hold district court. That street there is Rock Island Avenue. We'll
camp about ten or twelve miles southwest of town, on a creek that
drains into the South Canadian River. Four of us will go into town;
two will stay in camp. Here is about where that will be . . ."

He scratched a wiggly line well below the town; the line represented the South Canadian. A second line, drawn roughly perpen-
dicular to the first, was the creek where we would camp.

"The two who stay behind will have fresh horses saddled and
ready to go. Those horses we still must acquire, and they'll have to
be much stronger and faster than any of the nags we have here. The
four who go in will go in twos, one pair approaching from one end of
town, one pair from the other. We'll tie our horses up at the hitch
rails one store each side of the bank. We'll go inside two at a time.
Three will deal with the teller, or whoever is in there, and the vault;
one will watch the outside. When it's over, we'll hightail it out of town
together, going first in a false direction to fool any posse that comes
after us, then turning toward our camp and fresh horses the minute
we decide it's safe to do so."

He looked up, eyeing each of us in turn. When nobody said
anything, he went on, "We'll wear blue bandannas around our

necks. Inside the bank, and during our getaway, they'll cover our faces. We'll call ourselves by name just enough that everyone in there will be sure and hear them at least once, but not so that we overdo it. The names we'll use will be Bob, Emmett, Grat, and Bitter Creek. Juice, you'll be Bitter Creek again, because he's the only one as little as you . . ."

There seemed to be no end to the details of it. We talked well into the night and still more the next morning over breakfast. Janie and I were to be in charge of the fresh horses and the camp, thus missing the main action. I had to confess even then that I wasn't sorry about that. I wasn't a fully qualified outlaw yet; no one was convinced to that extent.

Kansas, Buster, and Juice would be in charge of acquiring the extra horses. It would be no small task and would have to be done among the first order of things. It would also have to be done before we left the hideout on the North Canadian. Clyde didn't want us doing anything stupid—like bringing attention to ourselves by sneaking into someone's horse pasture close at hand. And he didn't want any more Indian ponies. Something with a bit of thoroughbred blood and plenty of stamina would be good. It was decided that if they had to go all the way to Kansas, then that's what they would do. Three days were allotted for the chore, and seven horses—one to be used as a packhorse—were the number needed. Whether they were to be bought or stolen, I really didn't know, only that the three men rode out at midmorning, headed north and promising to be back within the time allotted.

And then there was the matter of certain supplies we were so often short of—food staples, mostly. When it came to making our getaway, traveling light but adequately provisioned for several days on the trail was of paramount importance. We wouldn't be visiting towns or farms or anything else where our needs could be fulfilled until we were well away from the scene of our crime, possibly even out of Oklahoma Territory. Clyde was inclined toward a trip on up the North Canadian to the town of Woodward, possibly even before the threesome who had gone for horses were back in camp.

Our getaway route would be roughly directed at southwestern Oklahoma, Texas, and eventually New Mexico or beyond. Clyde was adamant in his feeling that the haul this time would make it worthwhile to leave Oklahoma for good. He was almost visionary about it—the long-awaited strike at last! He was certain it would be so.

As for me, well, I just don't know what I was thinking. I certainly didn't have any illusions about successful outlaws, and I knew I had no business wanting to become any kind of one. There was only one reason I did what I did, and that reason was Janie. I was in love with her. I had this crazy hope that the big strike really would be big enough to be their last. I desperately desired that for Janie, and was willing to buy into it on the chance that there might somehow be a place in her life for me. . . .

That night, my mind was churning as I tossed inside my bedroll. A dozen yards away, beyond the campfire, Clyde snored. The fire had almost died and there was no moon, just millions of stars in a crystal-clear sky. A very light breeze caused leaves to flutter in the cottonwoods, and cicadas maintained an omnipresent din that was very difficult for one to ignore. I never felt so little inclined toward sleep in my life.

Finally I gave up. Quietly kicking loose from my bedroll, I sat up and tugged on my boots. Clyde did not stop snoring and Janie, who never snored, remained still in her bedroll. I rose and walked as softly as I could away from camp, down toward the river. It was pitch dark, and only the fifty or sixty trips I had taken along that same little path during the past few days qualified me to negotiate the distance without stumbling. I couldn't even make out the water in the river until I was practically at its edge.

For several moments I just stood there. Finally I reached down and found a rock. I tossed it out into the water and heard it splash.

It was no mystery, why I couldn't sleep. The more I considered the gang's bank-robbing plans, the more sobering I found my involvement in them. I wasn't about to back out, but it was becoming awfully clear to me how serious a business this was. People got shot at and chased and either killed or sent to prison for doing such things. And of course there was always the matter of right and wrong.

I was about to plunk another rock into the river when a noise at my back caused me to turn. A slender figure stood not five yards away.

"Janie! What are you doing here?"

"I was about to ask you the same thing," she said. "Is something wrong?"

"I couldn't sleep, is all."

She came on up to stand beside me and stare at the blackness of the river. "I couldn't either. I heard you leave, and I even wondered if maybe you were going to run away."

I stared at her. "What made you think that?"

"Well, it wouldn't be terribly difficult, you know. Clyde's not watching you the way he once did. Sneak a horse, and you could be in Woodward almost before we knew you were gone."

I hadn't thought about trying to escape for so long the idea actually startled me. "Well, that's not what I was doing," I said, a bit stiffly. "I never even considered it. Did you really think I might?"

"No, not really. I often wish you would, though."

"Why?"

"You know why."

"If I did, would I ask?"

"Probably."

I sighed. "Well, that's not the way it is. I see no reason you should wish me gone. No reason."

"Then you are a dumbhead, T.G. Shannon. I am thinking only of your welfare."

"Thanks," I said. "My mother will appreciate your timing. What is it now—almost six weeks since I was kidnapped by this gang?"

She didn't look at me. She just kept staring out across the river. "That's not fair, T.G. You know it isn't."

"Yeah, well . . ." I mumbled. "Okay, so it isn't. I know why you said it. This is all bad for me. Outlawry, you . . . especially you . . ."

She faced me then, her eyes locked on mine. "That's right. Especially me. I've told you that before. I *warned* you!"

"And you thought that would do any good? You actually thought that?"

She studied me. Finally she shook her head. "No. No, I guess not." She paused. "Do you love me, T.G.?"

"Yes."

"Are you sure? Really sure?"

I shrugged. "I can't remember ever being more sure about anything."

For a moment we were both silent. Finally I said, "Well?"

"I . . . don't know what to say, T.G. I truly don't."

"Say how you feel about me," I suggested. "About *us*."

She turned away again. "I'm not sure about that."

"About what? About which?"

"Either," she said weakly.

"I think you are. I think you just don't want to say."

"Are you sure you want to hear the answer, T.G.? Can you accept it if it's not what you wanted to hear?"

"I can if it's true."

She squared her shoulders and stared once more at the river. Her tone of voice seemed unnatural, forced. "I think you're a nice boy, T.G., much too nice to be mixed up in this business here. I think our kidnapping you may be the worst thing that ever happened to you, and I wish we had never held up that train of yours. I think Buster and I should have let you escape that first time you tried, back at that cave near the Arkansas. I think I should help you right now to steal a horse and get on out of here. I think—"

I just couldn't let her go on. I took her by the shoulders and forced her to turn toward me. But her head was down and she wouldn't look up. "I said the truth, Janie. Tell the truth."

"I was telling the truth. I—"

"Not all of it," I insisted. "Not the whole truth."

Finally she looked up. I couldn't be entirely sure, but I thought there were tears. "T.G., please don't make me say any more. Please don't."

I actually felt myself trembling, my heart racing. "Janie, you have to. It means too much to me. I *have* to know."

She gave a little shudder. Her shoulders relaxed and she let her arms go around me as she leaned against my chest. "Oh, T.G., what are we going to do? I don't want to lose you, yet I don't want to ruin your life either. I don't want you to become an outlaw. I wish to God we could both just run away from here right now. But I don't know if it would be the right thing for you; if I am right for you. I can't abandon my brothers—not now, not right in the middle of what they are planning to do in El Reno."

"And I won't leave unless you do," I said. "You know that, too, of course."

She responded with a reluctant nod. "I've known that for quite a while. I tried to pretend otherwise, but the longer you were with us, the more obvious it became." She looked up. "Oh, T.G., what a mess this is! What are we going to *do*?"

I gazed into those beautiful eyes and as gently as I knew how wiped the tears from each cheek with one finger. "When it's over— the big strike or no—then will you leave? Regardless of what Buster and Clyde do, will you give it up then?"

"I'm . . . not sure, T.G. I'm just not sure . . ."

"Why? For God's sake, why?"

"What would we do, you and I? Where would we go?"

"Well, I suppose we could go almost anywhere, just so long as it's well away from here. On west maybe, possibly even as far as California or Oregon, the way you've always planned. We could be married, live a normal life, raise kids . . . you know what I mean."

"What about your family? Would you never want to see them again?"

"Oh, sure, I would—someday, as soon as things are right for it. For the time being, I can just write to them so they'll know I'm okay."

Still she was hesitant. "I don't know. I just don't know."

"Look, at me, Janie," I said. "Look at me and tell me just one thing. Do you love me?"

"Oh, T.G., you know already. You know . . ."

"Say it. I want you to say it."

"Yes, then, damn you! Yes, yes, *yes*!"

My stomach was suddenly fluttering wildly inside. "Then say you agree. Tell me you'll leave with me when El Reno is over."

"Clyde might not let us," she worried. "He might not let either of us."

"Then we won't tell him. We won't tell any of them. We'll leave a note when we go. I won't be a bumbler about escaping this time. Honest, I won't."

She shook her head. "Oh, T.G., I still don't know . . ."

"Say yes, Janie. You said you love me. Didn't you mean it?"

Her eyes met mine in final resignation. She sighed, "Okay, T.G. As God is my witness, I must be crazy, but yes! I'll go with you wherever you say!"

Our faces were within inches of each other when I realized very belatedly that we had never so much as kissed. I did not let that oversight continue to ride for even one moment more.

CHAPTER 16

CLYDE awoke the following morning determined to make the trip to Woodward that day. We could make it there and back in two days or less, and would then be ready to head for El Reno as soon as the boys got back with the extra horses. As we saddled our horses, Janie stole a self-conscious look or two at me that I'm sure had to do with the night before, but Clyde never seemed to know that we had been away from our bedrolls, nor did he seem to notice anything different about us that morning.

By eight o'clock we were on our way, leading our one packhorse and figuring approximately a twenty-mile ride to our destination. We struck the main road that came from Cantonment and stayed with it all the way. I don't think we met over half a dozen parties the entire trip, and in every case Clyde simply smiled, tipped his hat, and chatted however long the other party wanted to before passing on. He didn't seem one bit worried to be out in the open the way we were. He said no one would suspect us of anything in particular way out there at the far end of nowhere, and there certainly was no reason to *create* suspicion by sneaking along in avoidance of the road.

Woodward stands but a short distance south of the North Canadian River. It wasn't much of a town before the 1893 opening of the Cherokee Strip, but its residents were accustomed to seeing strangers coming and going and we made our appearance without attracting any undue attention.

One reason for this is that Clyde didn't take many chances. From the time we left our camp on, he had Janie putting her hair up beneath her hat and wearing an oversized shirt and keeping her mouth shut around strangers so she could pass for his younger brother. I was supposed to be another brother, and we were all supposed to be cowpunchers put out of work by the military's campaign against the cattlemen. Judging from people's reaction to this, we couldn't have invented a more believable or timely tale if we had wanted to.

We bought our supplies without fanfare or incident, despite the fact that our purchases included a noticeable amount of ammunition to fit the various calibers of the gang's weapons. I hadn't thought we would be much short of that item, but Clyde wanted to be sure that enough and more was on hand.

"You don't go off unprepared in that department, T.G.," he told me as we loaded our packhorse outside the store. "Anything but that."

We camped that evening on the river about three miles from town, mostly to avoid unnecessarily overdoing our horses. The next morning we were back on the road we had traveled the day before, and by early afternoon were back at our camp on the North Canadian. It was an uneventful trip, but was much better than lying around camp for two days with nothing to do but wait for the rest of the gang to return.

"They oughta be here by tomorrow at the latest," Clyde predicted, "which should be just about right. I figure this is the twenty-second of July. I give us tomorrow to rest up and three full days to get to the new camp on the South Canadian. I'd really like to shoot for the morning of the twenty-seventh to do the job on that El Reno bank."

"Don't you think that's crowding it a bit?" I asked. "I mean, what if the boys don't show up until late tomorrow? That's sure not much rest for them."

He looked at me like a patient father. "Crowding it is the best way, T.G. It never pays to dawdle over these deals. It makes you hesitant and doubtful when you oughta be anything but. When it comes to robbing banks and trains, I figure those are the traits most likely to get you killed."

Kansas, Buster, and Juice—driving seven fine horses before them —burst upon the camp almost on cue about midmorning the following day. They followed the horses down a bluff, screeching and yelling like Sioux warriors returning from a raid. They ran the horses straight through camp (not entirely on purpose) and upset things there so badly they had Janie beside herself with anger.

We cornered and then caught the horses with lariats and soon built a small corral out of ropes strung between trees to hold them. They were all dark-colored animals—bays, chesnuts, and one black —and they were definitely blooded.

"Well, what do you think?" a dusty-faced Kansas wanted to know as we all stood surveying the haul.

"Where'd you get them?" Clyde asked.

"A horse ranch west of Kiowa, Kansas. First time in my life I've been in Kansas—ain't that something?"

Clyde's eyes narrowed. "Was there any trouble?"

"Not a bit," Kansas assured him. "There must have been forty horses in that pasture. No telling when these were even missed."

"How about on the way back? Nobody saw you driving them? No sign of anyone giving chase?"

Kansas grinned. "Don't worry so much, Clyde. Hell, we were careful. Besides, the Cherokee Strip is a mess just now. Deputy U.S. marshals are so busy arresting timber thieves on the Cimarron they hardly have time for simple outlaws. And the army's got itself twisted in a knot trying to force cattlemen out of the area. I don't think a soul paid us any mind. What do you think, Buster?"

"Didn't seem to," the younger Crosby brother said absently from nearby. "Say, Clyde, I sure do like that chestnut over there, the one with the blaze face. Think I'll pick him as mine. When'll we be leaving for El Reno? In about a week?"

Clyce smiled thinly. "A week? Hardly that, little brother, hardly that. Tomorrow is when we leave. First thing tomorrow."

"Aw, come on," Buster moaned. "You can't mean that. I was planning on resting up for a few days first. You gotta be joshing me, for crying out loud!"

"Tomorrow," Clyde repeated resolutely.

"I don't believe it," Buster carried on. "I just plain don't believe that, Clyde."

Clyde just said as he turned to walk away, "Tomorrow."

Clyde was boss. There was no further dissension among the gang. We spent the balance of the day resting, checking our gear, cleaning weapons, repairing tack, and in general discussing the plans for the job. I couldn't believe how calm all of them were about the undertaking. I was nervous as a declawed cat over it, and growing worse all the time. And I was to be only a horse-holder. These fellows were going to ride straight into a busy town and hold up its main bank. No telling what might happen; they might even get shot. Certainly they would be chased, which is where Janie and I could get dragged into the danger. Maybe they were just too dumb to be scared. I don't think so, though. They were a pretty nervy lot. To this day, I must give them and their kind that. A nervy lot.

That evening at sundown I helped Janie wash the supper dishes down at the river, and I asked her, "Aren't you scared? At least nervous?"

"Yes," she said. "I am."

"Which?"

"Both."

"Well, Clyde and the boys don't seem that way. They act about as excited as a roundup crew fixing to begin the spring works."

"They're different, T.G. They figure this is their line of work. It's not the same at all for them."

I wagged my head. "Doesn't sound like something they'll be willing to give up after the big strike. Sounds more like something they'll be compelled to just keep on doing."

She had been scrubbing a skillet rather diligently, but at my words she stopped and looked up sadly. "I've been a long time admitting that possibility to myself. You know how badly I want to think otherwise. I just hope you are wrong, T.G. Dear God, how I hope that you are."

The sun was gone behind the horizon now and the sky in the west glowed pale orange. We finished with the dishes but were not inclined to leave the river. We simply sat on the bank, gazing at the water.

Presently, the circumstances of our being there caused me to recall a certain experience that had weighed heavily on my conscience ever since it had happened. That I had kept it to myself for so long made me feel deceitful and ashamed. I knew I could never feel right about it unless a confession was made.

I asked Janie, "Do you remember that time we camped on that little creek that drains into the Arkansas—that first night after we left the cave in Osage country?"

"Yes," she said, looking at me quizzically. "What about it?"

"It was the night you went to the creek to bathe and the gang talked me into going down to wash dishes while you were gone."

She looked warily suspicious. "I remember that."

"We wound up across the creek from each other in the dark, you trying to find your clothes and me doing dishes and talking to you while you looked."

She said, "Go on."

"At first it was too dark to see a thing, but then the moon rose. It was the reason you finally found your shirt . . ."

Her eyes all but bored holes in me. "And . . . ?"

For just an instant I felt too panicky to go on with it. But then I shook myself, knowing it was too late to back out now. "Yours wasn't the only eyesight that was improved by the moonlight, Janie. It . . . was almost like day . . ."

I don't think she was too surprised at this point, but her voice was not its usual tone as she said, "I don't think I want to hear any more of this, T.G. I really don't."

"Well," I said resignedly, "I don't reckon there is much more. You know what I saw. I looked away afterward, but too late. I'm sorry, Janie. I've felt bad about it ever since. I guess I just couldn't go on without telling you."

I must have looked pretty crestfallen, because after a moment she actually began to seem sympathetic. She also seemed thoughtful. "You know, T.G., if I had any doubts at all that you love me, I guess I don't after this. I don't think you could have told me that, otherwise."

My misery eased somewhat. "You mean you aren't mad at me? You *forgive* me?"

She smiled thinly. "Well, I may have to think a bit about that . . ."

"Janie!"

She laughed and said, "Oh, all right, I forgive you. I mean, after all, it's not like that will be the only time you ever see me . . ." Even in the bad light, I could see that she was blushing mightily. "I mean . . ."

I was so relieved I almost missed her meaning. And then it dawned on me. Before I knew it she was in my arms, and I held her for several moments, neither of us saying anything. Presently I realized she was very softly crying. I leaned back and forced her to let me have a look at her. "Hey, what's this?"

I never saw eyes so solemn, even when tear-filled. "Oh, T.G., I'm just so afraid something will happen to make me lose you, that we will part ways somehow. You've all but made me forget my one great heartbreak in life — as much as anyone ever can. I just don't want to go through another one like it."

"Why, Janie," I said, startled. "What makes you think anything will happen to me?"

She just looked at me. She didn't have to say it — I knew. "Promise me, T.G., promise me you won't do anything foolish if we get caught by a posse or something. You won't fight them. You mustn't. You can't behave like my brothers and the other two. Please promise me, T.G."

I took her by the shoulders. "Janie, listen to me. You're all that counts with me. There is no way I'll let anything happen to either of us, no way we'll be parted. Believe me, it'll be all right. I swear it will."

We rode out from what was to prove our last real hideout shortly past sunup the next morning. Clyde had us up and breaking camp so early we were stumbling into each other, and it was clear that he was going to be all business until the bank job at El Reno was over. He kept going over each of our planned roles in the escapade till we were weary to the point of screaming. We didn't scream, though. We just said, "Yes, Clyde. I've got it, Clyde. I won't forget, Clyde."

Each of us had his or her extra horse assigned — by Clyde, of course. We led that horse and rode whatever one we had been riding before. Clyde and Kansas, in addition, led the packhorses, the second of which was a spare and would be saddled with pack only after the El Reno part of the operation was over.

We rode at a steady but unforced pace. Clyde and Kansas took the lead, while Buster and Juice rode side by side behind them. Janie and I brought up the rear. We lagged just far enough behind that we could talk freely, but not enough so as to create suspicion.

"Do they know anything?" I asked Janie. "Do they even suspect about us?"

She shrugged. "I'm not sure. Usually I can read Clyde better than I've been able to of late, and usually he can read me like a book. But he's been distracted by this El Reno thing, and I guess so have I."

"By the El Reno thing?"

She smiled. "No, you dope. By you! And I don't know how any of the others could have missed much. You're such a moon-eyed goose sometimes!"

"Jeez," I moaned. "Does it show that much?"

She laughed lightly. "Well, it does to me."

I moaned again.

We traveled openly, almost brazenly, and I suppose we were rather lucky not to encounter anyone smart enough to pay our rather suspicious-looking cavalcade any mind. We met and passed three wagons, probably nesters, and came within sight of at least a couple of Cheyenne or Arapaho camps located within sight of the road. Folks seemed in a mood to mind their own business in all cases.

For each of the first two nights we made creek-bottom camps along tributaries to the North Canadian. The farther we went, however, the more careful we became about who saw us on the road. Along about two o'clock the third day, we took cover in a wooded area of the North Canadian valley, the idea being to hole up for the rest of the day. At that point, we were no more than five miles from Fort Reno, and Clyde said we would head on south to our intended camping spot near the South Canadian beginning a little before nightfall.

"From now on, we make every effort not to be seen by anybody," he told us.

Shortly past sundown, we were on our way again. Our only real problem turned out to be finding the right creek on the South Canadian. Clyde had a pretty astounding sense of direction, however. Even with no moon, just stars and a relatively few landmarks to guide us, he always seemed to know where he was going.

By maintaining that same steady pace we had used all along, we reached our destination well before midnight. We made a fireless camp, tended our horses, and spread out our bedrolls. It had been a long day and we were tired. We would be up early next morning, for those going into El Reno had another ten- or twelve-mile ride ahead of them. But there was no talk of putting it off for another day. The gang was keyed up, ready. No one wanted to wait.

I don't know about the others, but I hardly slept a wink all night. Even if I was to do no more than help hold the horses several miles from the scene of action, the upcoming adventure promised to be the most eventful of my young life thus far, bar none.

CHAPTER 17

BASED largely on the way they later told it themselves, I know how it happened when the gang rode into that town the next morning. It was the twenty-seventh of July and a bright, fair day. They left Janie and me in the gray light of dawn, fully instructed as to our part in the affair. We knew almost precisely when to expect them back if all went well; we knew how long to wait if they did not return on schedule; we knew what to do in order to be ready for them when they came, and when to do it. We were just as ready as they were.

Clyde rode over to where I stood as they prepared to leave. "I hope you don't get any foolish ideas, boy. You've said where you stand in this thing and I've chosen to trust you in a pretty big way. I'm leaving you here with my sister and these horses that are so important to our getaway. You haven't the thought in mind of a double-cross, I hope."

I only said, "You're right, Clyde. I've said where I stand. I don't go back on my word."

For a long moment he studied me. "Good," he finally said, flashed his buck teeth, and reined his horse away. We watched the gray light and the trees envelop them and felt just a bit like a pair of rowboats cut loose in a fog.

They rode horses that should have been given more rest but that had to serve only for the one last ride and the ride back. The fresh horses that would await them were expected to more than outdistance any posse's already fading mounts. Their pace was easy but ground-gaining, their hope to hit El Reno at just the right time of day—when the place was in an unsuspecting rush to get its normal routine underway.

As it turned out, when they arrived the streets of the place were crowded with people and horses and wagons. As planned, two men rode in from one end of town, two from the other. Teamed together were Clyde and Buster, Kansas and Juice. Their horses were not lathered; they had been expertly saved for what was to come, for a time when they quite possibly could not be spared at all.

Arriving first, one store short of the bank, were Clyde and Buster. They stopped at a hitch rail, dismounted in a leisurely way, and looked on down the street as they tied up. Kansas and Juice could be seen about a block away, riding at a walk behind a teamster's freight wagon.

Leaving their rifles on their saddles, Clyde and Buster mounted a newly constructed boardwalk and surveyed the scene around them. It was not an idle survey. Anything at all untoward would have attracted their attention; anyone watching them, anyone even remotely resembling the law.

After a minute or so, they turned toward the bank and mingled with others walking along. They talked and laughed and let themselves be overheard remarking how good it would be to have a night on the town later on. By and large, they were ignored.

They stopped in front of the bank and looked back across the street. No one seemed to notice the slight bulge beneath Buster's jacket that was a carefully folded burlap grain sack to be used in the bank. Nor did their blue neckerchiefs and dusty clothes make them stand out in the crowd. They could easily have just been a couple of cowpunchers lolling there.

Not far away, Kansas and Juice tied their horses to a post at the edge of the street. They too took their time, looking all around. It seemed to go unnoticed that they also wore blue neckerchiefs and that Kansas had a light bulge beneath his jacket similar to Buster's. They also left their rifles on their saddles as they turned to the walk.

They were still a dozen yards away, Juice hobbling slightly behind Kansas, when Clyde and Buster turned and entered the bank, closing the door behind them. Moments later, Kansas and Juice followed suit.

Amazingly, there was only one other person inside—a woman, the cashier. She had just finished opening the vault and was about to begin counting money in the drawers behind the counter. Her surprise when she looked up and saw two, then four, masked men with guns drawn must have been surpassed only by her shock when one of them said:

"Emmett, Grat, over here. Bitter Creek, keep an eye on that door."

"Sure, Bob," one of them said.

Hands flying to her breast, the woman moaned, "Oh, my God, the Daltons!" and crumpled to the floor in a dead faint.

Clyde looked around, saw the open vault door, and said, "Well, I'll be damned."

He actually went over to see if the woman was all right as Kansas and Buster shook out their burlap bags and headed for the vault.

The gang did not close the curtains on the bank's front windows simply because they thought that would draw more outside attention than it would prevent. They were probably right about this, but it did leave them vulnerable to someone glancing in from the walk and figuring out what was going on. Fortunately for them, the windows were dust-covered and small, and it wasn't until two of them were coming out of the vault that someone finally did look through and see them. That person, a woman, immediately turned to her companion, another woman, and exclaimed, "My God, there are men in there wearing masks! They must be robbing the bank!"

At this hard-to-believe revelation, the second woman decided to have a look for herself. She was standing there, her face plastered against the window pane, when Juice noticed her.

"Hey, fellows, I think we've been found out. Better hurry it up."

Kansas and Buster were in the process of carrying one bag filled with paper currency and another half full of coins from the vault. Clyde had found a smaller bag somewhere and was busy emptying the drawers behind the cashier's cage. Outside, the lady at the window suddenly pulled away, looking horrified. Those inside could hear her shriek even with the doors closed.

"Come on," Clyde said. "Let's go!"

They burst through the doors and onto the walk, guns drawn and masks still covering their faces. For a moment the busy street scene hardly seemed to change. The two ladies were halfway to the opposite stide of the street by then, babbling incoherently to anyone who would listen and pointing back the way they had come. The few who seemed to have taken notice of them looked mostly confused. Those on the walk nearby were slow to react. When any of them finally did do something, it was nothing very threatening to the bank robbers. Most saw six-guns being waved around and ducked for cover. One or two simply froze in terror. No one moved to interfere. Quickly the four men separated and headed for the horses. But for the hobbling-slow Juice, they might very well have made it out of town without a shot being fired at them.

Clyde and Buster reached their horses first and were mounted, waiting, while Kansas and Juice were still making their way down the walk. Clyde carried the fuller of the two money sacks, the one carrying paper currency, while Buster had charge of the smaller bag filled with what had been gleaned from the cash drawers. Kansas toted the one containing coin. Juice, trying to run, twice stumbled and almost fell. Kansas's horse attempted to bolt as they approached, probably shying at the bag Kansas carried. Juice belatedly arrived in time to hold the bag while Kansas mounted, then went through a small rodeo of his own trying to contain his own mount.

All in all, the time it took for all four men to leave the bank and mount up should scarcely have amounted to a minute. With Juice lagging behind it took almost two — not much time, by most standards, but plenty for the paralysis in the street to begin to wear off.

Even before the first of the outlaws had reined around to start his dash from town, shots rang out. Return fire echoed and more bystanders darted for cover. A man with the look of the law in his actions came running down the street. Others, equally determined, followed. They were coming from the direction of the jail, and only later did I learn that district court was in session nearby and that at least one of these men was a deputy U.S. marshal, there to testify in various cases in which he had been an arresting officer. With Clyde leading the way, the four outlaws stormed back up the street, bullets flying after them but miraculously none connecting.

They made one turn, down a side street going west. Once clear of the town, they made another turn, this time angling mostly south but still somewhat west. They had hopes of at least masking the true direction of their flight. But even a while later, when they began to reach somewhat broken country and felt themselves well out of sight, they still did not tarry or slow down. They sensed that their pursuit might be a hot one, and they were not wrong in thinking that.

The posse that would follow them out of El Reno would take a full half hour to form, but it would be composed of at least one professional and a very determined group of followers who thought they were chasing the Daltons.

What none of us knew until much later—and the most astounding fact of all to me—was that my brother Sam rode with that posse. This came about more by chance than anything else. Sam had been in Indian and Oklahoma Territories for almost a month at the time, writing home every chance he got to keep or ma and the others posted as to his progress. All had been pretty discouraging since that day in the Triangle when that posse he was with had almost captured us. He was convinced that the youth described to him by that old man Clyde had let go had been me. His disappointment had been considerable when they failed to come up with me, but he was no longer discouraged. Like a hunter who had finally seen and just missed his deer, he was fired with renewed enthusiasm for the hunt.

Trouble was, no one had known for sure who the gang they were chasing was. That old man who had claimed to know the Daltons might have known the brothers themselves, but he didn't know everyone in the gang. For all he knew, we could have been Doolin, Newcomb, Pierce, Powers, Broadwell, and maybe that girlfriend Bob Dalton supposedly consorted with from time to time. His descriptions of us to the various posse members had been totally inconclusive. That we might have been certain members of the Dalton gang simply could not be ruled out.

Whoever we were, what mattered to Sam was that the posse had missed us. He didn't even know how really close they had come, for when the gang and the posse had split up, no one could be sure which way I—if I were present at all—had gone. The half of the posse Sam was with had spent a week after losing us trying to relocate our trail, but again only failure had resulted. They had finally disbanded, and a disconsolate Sam had been left with nothing to do but follow a couple of deputy marshals, first to Guthrie, and later to El Reno.

Needless to say, there were rewards out, mostly from my express company and the railroad, to anyone affecting my rescue, the capture of the outlaws, or both. Not many around El Reno seemed interested in this, however, except perhaps the two deputy marshals, who at the time were waiting around to give testimony in district court and could not leave. Because of this, Sam had been in town five days, trying unsuccessfully to interest someone in organizing another posse to hunt for me, when the bank holdup occurred.

I suppose it was fated that one of the two deputies had completed his testimony early the morning of the El Reno holdup and was simply hanging around outside the courtroom when the Crosby gang burst from the bank after making that poor woman inside think they were the Daltons. It didn't take long for the woman to revive and begin telling people that, and it took even less time for the deputy marshal to begin forming a posse. I doubt if he was a bit surprised to find Sam his very first volunteer.

During all this, Janie and I sat beneath a heavily branched walnut tree, avoiding the late morning sun. The creek, spring fed, trickled in front of us. Just downstream—about half a mile—it joined the South Canadian River. Across the creek, our relief horses stood tied to various bushes, ready and waiting to be saddled. Janie had fixed up some light lunches of meat and bread for us and the boys to eat as soon as the latter arrived. It was hoped that they would not be so closely pursued that we would have to forego the meal, but of course we were prepared for that possibility.

We were prepared, but we were also as nervous as a couple of tame town cats left stranded in a barnyard. It had been the longest morning of our young lives. We had busied ourselves as best we could, but by far our main chore was to simply sit and wait. Nothing could have been harder.

"We should have bought some grain for those horses when we were in Woodward," I remarked as I watched the one assigned to me nibble on a branch.

"I know. Clyde thought of it too late, only after Buster and the boys came back with them. But it won't matter. Those animals are still the equal of any posses' horses I ever saw."

I looked at her. "Does the prospect of being chased by another posse frighten you?"

Without looking at me, she nodded. "I never was before, not like this. I'm just so afraid something won't work out . . . . Do you know what I mean?"

I did, but I wasn't about to encourage any gloomy thinking. I said, "It'll work out, Janie. Just believe that, will you?"

She fell silent and for several minutes we just sat there. Finally I pulled out my watch. "It's about time we saddled the packhorse, don't you think?"

A short while later we watched them coming, four riders in a bunch, from a rise located just beyond the trees that surrounded our creek-bottom camp. We had ridden up there hoping to get just such a look at them, and thus some forewarning as to their arrival. The country they were crossing was generally open but somewhat rolling. They were at least a mile away, coming fast. We had waited on that rise a good half hour and were becoming pretty edgy when at last they had come into view.

Janie instantly jumped up from where she had been sitting in front of her ground-reined horse. "It's them! I know it is!"

I rose beside her, squinting hard. My own horse nibbled at sparse grass a few yards away. I said. "They're coming hell-for-leather all the way. Do you see anyone chasing them?"

"No . . . I don't think so. Only them."

"Maybe we ought to go on back to camp and wait for them."

She put a hand on my arm before I could turn. "Wait—let them get closer. I think we should try to be sure they are not being followed. We may be able to see something they cannot."

I agreed without argument. Even as we watched, the pace of the four riders seemed to slow, their horses probably flagging. Presently they went out of sight in a depression in the landscape—a dry creek bottom with few trees. Janie and I searched from horizon to creek bottom and saw nothing of any pursuers.

In a couple of minutes, the first rider reappeared. The other three followed close behind, coming on at what seemed a labored gallop.

I said to Janie, "Are you satisfied now? Can we go?"

Somewhat reluctantly she pulled her gaze away and turned toward her horse. But even as we mounted and were about to ride away we dawdled for a last look back. And it was then that we saw something—in the distance beyond the oncoming gang—a hovering cloud of dust. Beneath the dust, tiny specks began to appear. They looked like a sizable bunch of riders, and they were coming our way.

I said, "Oh-oh."

And Janie replied, "Do you see what I was talking about? Do you *now*?"

CHAPTER 18

WE found the camp and our relief horses just as we had left them. It was a good thing. A few minutes later the gang rode up on lathered mounts that were completely exhausted. I don't think those poor animals could have gone a foot farther. They stood with heads hanging and sides heaving as their saddles were stripped from them and their bridles removed. Janie and I noticed immediately the sacks of loot a couple of them had been carrying in addition to their riders.

"Do you know you are being chased?" Janie asked Clyde.

"Yeah," he said. "We saw them back there a couple of times. I figure we've got over a half hour on them, though. With our fresh horses to their worn-out ones, that should be plenty of time."

"Are we going to split up or stay together?" she asked then, both possibilities having been discussed during the planning step of the job.

He shrugged. "It's normal to count out the money and divvy up before we separate. We don't have time for that now. I'd say we stay together for a while yet. Maybe we'll lose that posse and won't have to split up at all."

Janie considered this, then said, "I fixed you some lunches. Will you have time for them?"

Buster looked up from the saddling of a fresh horse. "Will we have *time* for them? By damn, we'll *make* time!"

"I echo that to the letter," Kansas put in.

I simply marveled at the lot of them. Here they were, having just robbed a bank of maybe the most money any of them would ever see, a posse hot on their trail, a probable desperation dash for freedom still ahead of them, and they were hungry. Even Janie seemed to have regained some steel. Already she was on her way to pass out the lunches.

But as always, it was Clyde who had the last word. He finished his saddling and made sure his bedroll was tied on fast behind his cantle, then turned to the rest of us.

"We'll eat as we ride," he said.

We hazed what were now our extra horses ahead of us. The four animals that had made the trip to El Reno and back that morning lagged behind, their stamina destroyed. Because of this, we couldn't go very fast, but Clyde insisted we at least cross the river with them, that confusion in our tracks could be gained that way.

We followed the creek to its confluence with the river but were greeted there with a poor place to cross. Sandbars and quicksand dominated the riverbed. The water was shallow, however, and not far upriver we found a decent crossing. We drove the seven horses out onto the opposite bank and watched them move away. We didn't expect them to go far, but had hopes that the posse would follow them for whatever distance that would be. When we ourselves left the river, we went one at a time over a stretch of about fifty yards of bank before finally coming together again to begin our dash in earnest.

From this point on that day, our confidence about our situation could only grow. Our horses were very fine animals, powerful and graced with stamina. We believed them capable of a pace that a posse on tired horses and having to stop and study tracks could not possibly maintain. We also used every ploy to cover our trail, from dragging limbs behind our horses to riding in among this and that small bunch of cattle. We took to rocky slopes wherever we could find them. We changed directions frequently. We rode up another creek bed, carefully staying in the water until we found the least likely place to exit and go on our way. Even very good trackers were going to have trouble with our trail.

Another thing in our favor: We were now in a country assigned to the Wichita, Caddo, and about half a dozen smaller tribes of Indians. Unlike the Cheyenne and Arapaho lands to the north and west of us, this area had not been opened for white settlement. They were wild lands of blackjack and good grass and deep canyons with high sandstone walls and pretty little creeks running down the canyon bottoms. Clearly, Clyde had known what he was doing when he had picked this as a getaway route.

Late that afternoon, we chose one of those canyons as a place to camp for the night. High rock walls rose several hundred feet on each side of us, while spreading walnut trees, lofty cottonwoods, thick plum thickets, a trickling stream, and a small waterfall characterized our closer surroundings. The spot was terrifically isolated, but it did give us pause in its selection because it could have served as a terrible trap if we were discovered there and surrounded. However, we had seen no sign of our pursuers since before our crossing of the South Canadian earlier in the day, and thus we considered the likelihood of our being discovered a slight one.

Because of the high walls, sundown came early in the canyon. Buster and I staked the horses out to graze while the others debated whether or not to make a fire.

Buster said to me, "You're in love with my sister, aren't you, T.G.?"

I was busy pounding a stake pin with a rock and almost smashed my hand. I looked up. "Is it *that* easy to see?"

He harrumphed. "Been pretty easy for a long time. Any fool could see that's the reason you've stayed the way you have. Hell, you think we're all stupid?"

I put a lot of apparent concentration into tying and testing a knot in the stake rope. "Why are you telling me this now?"

"Well, could be I've noticed Janie looking a little moon-eyed over you lately too. Could be I'm wondering if you two haven't made plans the rest of us don't know anything about."

"And if we have?"

Buster shrugged. "Depends. She's a grown girl. Just depends on what those plans are."

I sighed and said, "We haven't meant to be dishonest about it. I guess our plans depend a lot on what the gang does from here on. We're sort of counting on this being the last job, you know—the way Clyde said it would be."

Buster only said, "I see."

"This *is* going to be the last job, isn't it, Buster?"

He turned and started to walk away.

I hustled after him. "Answer me, Buster. Is it?

"I don't know."

"Why don't you know? Clyde has always said after the big strike . . . Isn't this it?"

He waved a hand as if shooing away a pesky fly. "We haven't counted the loot, yet. We don't know if it's that big or not."

I didn't like the sound of this at all. "Well, when will you count it? When will you know?"

"Pretty soon, I imagine. Pretty soon."

They had decided on a small fire so Janie could fry some and boil a pot of coffee to go with some cold bread left over from breakfast. Buster looked longingly toward the creek as I helped Janie gather wood for the fire.

"I wonder if there are any fish in that creek."

Kansas groaned and Clyde said, "Forget it, Buster. We eat, then we count out the money and divvy up. I want everybody to have his share in case something unexpected happens."

Not quite under my breath, I said, "Good."

"What's that, T.G.?"

"Oh, nothing. Just mumbling."

An hour later, beneath a fully darkened, moonless sky, we were gathered around a blanket beside the fire. Atop the blanket had been dumped a pile of greenbacks and coin. I was very much reminded of my first night with the gang, except this was a great deal larger pile of loot and an awful lot had changed about my life since then.

I sat between Janie and Clyde, the latter of whom looked at me and said, "We never voted you a share, T.G. It's up to the others here if they want to do that now."

Surprised, I stammered, "That . . . won't be necessary. I mean, I never expected . . ."

"I guess if he's bashful about it," Kansas suggested, "we could give him half a share. The rest of us could split the other half."

"Honest . . ." I said.

"You've been a good sport, T.G.," Clyde said. "I think a half share would be fair. We could split six ways, give you one-half of one-sixth and do as Kansas says with the rest."

Janie and I exchanged uncomfortable looks. I tried once more to protest. "I really don't think—"

"I'll go along with it," Buster interrupted. "Like Clyde says, it's only fair."

"Juice?" Clyde asked.

The little man grunted. "Yeah, sure. I ain't got no quarrel with it. Give it to him."

"Janie?"

She looked completely uncertain. She glanced once again at me, then said, "I really don't think T.G. . . . I mean, he . . . I . . ."

All eyes turned to me. I felt a bit overwhelmed. These men were outlaws. They had risked their lives for every penny on that blanket. All I had done was stay with Janie and the horses, tag along, not cause trouble.

"Look," I finally said. "This is a hell of a gesture. Even a log would be smart enough to appreciate it. But darn it, I just don't feel right taking anything. I'm just a novice here. I don't deserve it. I—"

Clyde cut me off. "Forget it. We've already voted. Janie, I reckon you've abstained, but the rest of us say yes. You get a cut, T.G., that's all there is to it."

And he was right; I could see that further argument would not only be useless but aggravating. To them, it would be like rejecting hospitality—something you just did not do in those days.

I sat and watched as they counted it out. It took a while—the take amounted to just slightly over ten thousand dollars in negotiables. I found it hard to conceive of so much. My cut, half of one-sixth, $835, was far more than I had ever owned at one time.

"What'll I do with it?" I asked Janie as we sat together before the fire after the others had drifted off to their bedrolls. "I mean, where will I put it? Clyde and the boys all have money belts and Clyde carries your share."

Her eyes were discerning, her voice kept low. "You didn't want it at all, did you, T.G.?"

"No, I didn't."

"I'm sorry. They were determined. You did right by not being stubborn."

"Yeah, well," I said, "that still doesn't tell me what I'm going to do with it."

She shrugged. "Keep it. Hide it in your bedroll. If you really don't want it, later we can figure out something to do with it."

"Later." I considered this. "When you and I leave the gang, Janie? Is that what you mean?"

Firelight danced on her troubled features as she spoke. "Yes. Then, I guess . . ."

"We *are* going to go our own way, aren't we?"

"Shhhh!" she whispered. "You're talking too loud!"

I looked around. The closest bedroll was Buster's, and that was two dozen yards away. Still, he was close enough to overhear. I lowered my voice. "You didn't answer me. Are we or aren't we?"

Her eyes darted toward the gang's bedrolls. "Please, T.G.," she pleaded. "This is not the time. Please!"

"Well . . ." Of course she was right.

"And besides, I am very tired. This has not been an easy day, you know."

I sighed. "Yeah, okay. I guess I'm tired, too." I rose and gave her a hand.

We stood there for just a moment before I said, "Well, good night . . ."

She let me just start to turn, then she stopped me. "T.G., trust me, will you? I do love you. Believe me, I do."

One look at her there in the firelight, a moment before she kissed me lightly and was gone, was all I needed to know that she did not lie.

The sun showed itself late in the canyon next morning, just as it had gone down early the day before. I guess that—and the fact that we had all been near exhaustion when we went to bed—was the reason we all overslept. I awoke about seven o'clock. Janie was the only one up, and she was just in the process of starting a fire.

I rolled out and started putting on my boots. While I was at this, Clyde stirred in his bedroll, then Kansas, and finally Juice and Buster.

Clyde wasn't very happy. "This is no good. We should have been long gone from here by now. If that posse's still on our trail, we've given them one hell of an opportunity to make a move on us."

We ate half-cooked bacon and burned our mouths trying to gulp our coffee down before Clyde had us saddling our mounts. We broke camp as if every U.S. marshal in two territories was about to burst upon us. If Clyde was being wisely cautious, the rest of us were only grumbling.

"God, I'm tired of this," Buster said. "Sleeping on the ground, wearing wore-out clothes, stinking from the lack of a bath, eating out of tin plates, bacon and bread, being hounded . . ."

Clyde wasn't sympathetic. "Complain away, little brother. Foreget all about how heavy that money belt is around your middle. Forget what you'd probably be doing if you weren't doing this: hanging out in some dingy cow camp somewhere or trailing along behind a dusty herd or cutting fence posts to sell to boomers. Forget all of that."

Buster let it drop.

We encountered some difficulty finding a way out of the canyon that would allow us to take the direction we wanted. When we finally discovered a way, we tried to go mostly west but wound up encountering another creek bottom, heavily wooded, and were more or less forced by steeper walls to follow it downstream. Directions were hard to keep; I think we must have angled mostly south, soon finding the confluence of the one creek with another.

Two miles downstream on this one and we came to its mouth, where it drained into a much larger creek.

"I don't like this," Kansas said. "We're wasting time and not getting anywhere."

"At least we'll give a tracker fits," Buster allowed.

We crossed the larger creek and finally got our westward bearings. About noon, we came to a large expanse where both trees and grass had been burned, possibly during the previous winter. The grass had regrown and was green, but the trees were stark and dead. A short while later, we spotted some Indians on a far hill. Kansas thought they might be Cheyenne, although we were still in Wichita and Caddo country. They gave no indication of seeing us, but we were forced to steer to the northwest to avoid them.

Along about three o'clock, Juice complained that his horse was going lame. Somewhere along the way it had lost a shoe. The animal could still be ridden, but there was no way our pace would not be slowed considerably.

"Just what we needed," Clyde groaned. "No telling when or where we'll find a replacement for him."

"It's not my fault," Juice said. "I'm just riding him, not telling him where to put his feet."

Kansas said, "We're just lucky he's the only one it's happened to. These old ponies have covered a lotta miles in the last few days."

I guess we were all beginning to have our apprehensions by then, and we were doing an awful lot of looking back as we rode. So much so, I guess, that as we rode up a dry creek bottom in some thick trees we were surprised by a small group of cowhands driving a bunch of half-wild cattle. We nearly scattered their cows for them and had no way of avoiding a meeting with a pair of them who had been trailing along behind the herd.

The two left their buddies to handle the cows and rode over to where we had stopped. They looked us over with suspicious eyes, but seemed to know better than to ask anything.

"Just passing through," Clyde told them, then cast a purposefully suspicious gaze of his own toward the herd.

"We're not rustlers," one of the riders said. "We work for a Chickasaw rancher who used to lease this country from the Wichitas and Caddos. The Cheyennes stole him blind and made things so tough he gave up his lease. Last winter, they even started prairie fires, trying to burn him out. This is just a clean-up job to get what cows are left back home to Chickasaw territory."

We all remembered the burned-out country we had ridden through earlier and found no reason not to believe what the cowhand was telling us.

Clyde nodded and said, "Don't suppose you'd have any ideas where we could make a swap for this lame horse, here."

The two men eyed Juice's horse. The one who had spoken before said, "Well, this ain't settled country, I suppose you know. Not many places you can just go to swap horses. And don't be looking at none we have. We're darn near on foot as it is."

Clyde, for a moment, stiffened as if he were considering taking the man's horse whether he wanted to swap or not. Apparently he thought better of this, for he smiled and asked, "You sure you've got no other suggestions?"

"I don't suppose you'd consider using that packhorse there for a saddle mount," the man said.

Clyde shook his head in the negative. "And dump all our supplies and gear? No, we wouldn't want to do that. And this lame animal does us no more good carrying a pack than he does carrying a man. We need another horse, is all."

"Well, there is one other possibility," the man mulled. "This boss of mine built a headquarters for his lease country north of here near Deer Creek. Had a dugout there, some corrals, and a big horse pasture close by. Some of the best-bred horses in the territory were kept there. The Cheyennes were hell on them, though, just as they were the cows. More than once they scattered the whole herd and we never did regather all of them. Last I heard some were still running loose there. Now it's not that I'm advising horse theft, mind you, but my boss has pretty well given what's left of those animals up for lost. Catch one and leave yours, and I don't reckon anyone'd ever say much."

"How far to this Deer Creek?"

"No more'n ten miles. You can make it by dark or a little after, depending on how much that lame horse slows you up. I can draw you a map on the ground if you like."

We would have to turn north to reach Deer Creek, and after some discussion decided maybe it was worthwhile. We left the cowhands behind and set out in the prescribed direction. After about a mile, we stopped and looked back. The cowhands and their herd had left the creek bottom and were rapidly moving out of sight, going east.

"We didn't fool those fellows any," Kansas observed sagely.

Clyde shrugged. "Of course we didn't. There wasn't much use trying. But I believe what he told us about his boss's horses and the dugout headquarters. How's your horse, Juice?"

"'Bout had it. Much farther, and I'll be leading him."

"That would be something," Buster said. "You with your game foot leading a lame horse."

What happened was, I wound up letting Juice ride my horse, while he led the lame one and I rode double with Janie. Even with this, we did not make the best of time and it was almost sundown by the time we reached Deer Creek. We found no horses running loose, but after following the creek bottom upstream for about two miles, we came upon a tributary, coming in from the south, that fit to a tee the description of the one on which those cowhands had said the Chickasaw rancher had constructed his dugout. Trouble was, by then it was almost dark.

"I see no reason to go any farther tonight," Clyde said. "Deer Creek has good water in it; this tributary has ony a trickle. I say we camp here. Anybody disagree?"

Kansas said, "What about the horses that cowhand told us about? Where are they?"

"Beats me," Clyde said. "Maybe we made a poor gamble on that score. But it's too late to do anything about that now. I figure we make camp and if we don't find any horses in the morning, we'll just have to go on the way we have been and make the best time we can."

"But what if there's a posse back there?" Janie asked. "What if we have to run for it?"

"Well, that's a different matter, of course. We'll deal with that if it happens."

"What about the packhorse?" Kansas put in. "Maybe that cowhand was right. Let Juice switch to the packhorse and let the lame one carry the pack. That way, if we have to run we'll at least all be mounted on sound animals."

"We can do that, all right. But I sure would hate to lose that pack with all of our gear and supplies."

"It would only happen in an emergency, Clyde," Kansas assured him. "Only if we were really being pushed."

We voted to make camp. We had made awfully poor time during the day and I don't think anyone felt very comfortable about that. But the horses were tired and we were tired and food and rest were heavy on our minds. It hardly seemed that we had much choice.

Kansas said it best. "I reckon we've about gotta stop, all right. But I'd sure hate to think anybody's still on our trail. And I'd hate even worse to think they might have run into that bunch of cowhands by now and know *exactly* where we were going."

It's just too bad we were so right in worrying about that—and yet were so wrong in not worrying about it more.

CHAPTER 19

WE built a small fire and staked the horses out to graze along a grassy south bank of Deer Creek. Water trickled nearby with dim starlight — and that of a most slender sliver of moon — barely reflecting on its surface. Janie was frying bacon for supper and preparing sourdough to be baked for breakfast in a Dutch oven smothered in coals. Water was just coming to a boil in our coffeepot. The gang, myself included, sprawled here and there around the fire. The subject of the gang splitting up had again been broached.

Clyde said, "I've been thinking that we should, all right. I was even thinking we might do it first thing tomorrow. Of course I realize we've still got Juice's horse to worry about. But even if there are a bunch of that rancher's horses wandering loose in the neighborhood, I'm not sure how much time we can afford to spend trying to locate them. I'm betting if we were to push on west from here, we wouldn't go far before coming to settled country. I figure we're no more than a few miles from the Cheyenne-Arapaho line right now."

"Which are we going to do first?" Kansas asked. "Split up or go looking for a horse for Juice?"

"I think we should go ahead and split up," Clyde said. "Juice will just have to make do till something else shows up." Then he paused. "Kansas, I figure you and Juice will want to go together; Buster and Janie will stay with me —"

"Clyde!" Janie exclaimed. "You didn't say anything about T.G. You know I . . . how I . . ."

He wagged his head tiredly and looked at me. "And T.G. I guess you'll be wanting to stay with Janie. Am I right?"

I didn't know what to say. I only shrugged.

"Course, I've been meaning to ask you a few things about that,"

Clyde went on. "You and Janie. Any fool can see you two are all calf-eyed over each other, but no one's ever said what your intentions are. Tell me straight out: Do you plan to do right by my sister, soon as we're where you can?"

I straightened. "I've never done *wrong* by your sister, Clyde."

His expression did not change. "Well, it's some relief to know that, all right. But my question is, do you intend to marry her? Do you feel as strongly as that about her?"

"Yes. Yes, I do. Of course I do!" I looked around, embarassed.

Buster laughed. "Well, I've sure gotta hand it to you, T.G. You've come a long way since we first took you off that train. You started out our prisoner and now you're about to marry into the family and become one of us."

"Yeah, T.G.," Kansas said. "A real outlaw."

Janie tensed at my side. "T.G. is *not* an outlaw, Kansas. This is supposed to be our last job, remember? He's going along with it only because of me, and we—neither of us—want any more to do with it. If he's an outlaw, it's only because *we've* made him one."

This was greeted with a silence at least as dead as our campfire would be by morning.

Finally Clyde said, "There's a lot even you don't understand, Janie. I know what you say is true and have all along. But if a posse catches us with T.G. along, they may or may not be willing to believe he's so innocent. To them—and maybe a federal judge—an outlaw is liable to be an outlaw no matter how he came to be one."

Janie was rendered suddenly very subdued by this.

Clyde went on, "And I can make no promises as to our odds on getting away clean. Who knows what's ahead or behind us now? In this business, you always run the risk of something going wrong at the worst possible time. Just like that lame horse of Juice's, just like a lot of things could still go wrong."

This added solemnity to all our silences. When no one spoke, Clyde said, "Well, enough of that. Do we want to meet back up somewhere? I figure it can't be too soon—a month, maybe even six weeks. And it can't be too close to here or anyplace in Oklahoma. I've been thinking of either California or Oregon . . ."

I hardly slept that night. I simply could not stop thinking. I had this perfectly fateful feeling that things were not going to work out right, that the next day would provide not only an eventful time but an unhappy one as well.

I don't think Janie slept much either. Her bedroll lay across the campfire from mine, but I heard her tossing and turning throughout a good part of the night. Several times I considered getting up and going over to her, but something kept me from doing that. I guess it had to do with what I dutifully considered the impropriety of me going near her bedroll at night. In any case, I just lay there and suffered with my fuzzy sense of foreboding, dozing briefly a few times but wide awake mostly, until dawn when the others began to stir in their bedrolls.

"We'll eat first, but quickly," Clyde said as he shook himself out. "You rebuild the fire, T.G.; Janie, you get the coffee and the bacon going and serve up some of that bread. The rest of us will get the horses saddled and ready to ride."

The sun still hadn't risen when we finished eating, which was about the time we realized that the sky was more than half overcast. Clyde seemed unusually nervous, and I remember wondering if he had had a night similar to mine. He also evidenced some second thoughts about making Juice ride a lame horse.

"Juice can ride Janie's horse; Janie will ride double with T.G. and someone else can lead Juice's lame one," he instructed as someone kicked dirt over the fire and the rest of us checked our saddle girths.

There was amazing calm in the atmosphere just then, and I distinctly recall Buster saying, "Something don't feel right. It just sure as hell don't."

I mounted first and was about to reach down to give Janie a hand up behind me. I had removed my left foot from its stirrup and Janie was just in the process of lifting her foot to be put there when a voice rang out from somewhere within the trees and brush to our left.

"Hold it right there! All of you! This is Deputy U.S. Marshal Wheeler. You are all under arrest!"

What took place next happened so fast I hardly had time to think. Juice had been the one kicking out the fire, and thus was farthest from his horse and closest to the sound of the voice. The best I can figure, it just must have been the outlaw instinct not to submit to capture, to go instinctively for one's gun instead. At least that's what Juice did. I know he fired first—at what I'm not sure, probably just the general direction of the voice—but after that it seemed there was firing from everywhere around me, including the trees.

I had all I could do just trying to control my horse. At the first shot he shied and caused Janie, her foot not yet quite in the stirrup, to lose her balance and fall backward. He also whirled away from the trees whence most of the shooting was coming.

After that, most of my impressions became terribly fragmented and pain-filled. Just as I got control of the horse and was about to turn him back toward Janie, I felt a tremendous impact to my back, fairly high up around my left shoulder. There wasn't any pain at first, just a hard, numbing jolt. I guess it threw me forward, onto my horse's neck, for I remember having a face full of mane only seconds before the animal shied again, this time out from under me. I took another hard jolt to my back as I hit the ground, and a blinding flash of light was followed by sudden darkness.

Consciousness must have gone and come quickly during the next few moments. I remember someone being at my side and knowing, although I could see only a blur when I opened my eyes, that it was Janie, crying and saying my name over and over. Her hands fluttered at my shirt, then at my face, and then she seemed to try to hug me and pull my face to her breast.

But suddenly I heard Clyde's voice from close by. "You can't help him, Janie! Juice is down, too! We can't help either of them. Quick . . . get on that horse!"

And then she was being pulled away from me. I heard her still crying my name, but her voice became distant. The gunfire, if anything, seemed to grow in intensity. I heard someone yell, "They're getting away! Four of them are getting away!" I heard hoofbeats, more yelling . . . .

And then, over it all, I began to perceive a new voice, a familiar one, someone yelling. "Stop! For God's sake stop firing! That's my brother you've downed over there! *Stop firing!*"

And I blacked out again.

Someone was working over me, trying to talk to me. "T.G., can you hear me? If you can, please say something."

My brother Sam was a big, raw-boned man, not especially good-looking but kindly in both appearance and manner. Even in my condition, there was no mistaking his voice or his slightly blurry visage.

My mouth was dry and I hurt terribly. The sky seemed darkened, making me think—as if nothing else might—that death must be about to overtake me. Then I realized that I was beneath something —looking not at the sky at all but at the underside of a hastily built canvas lean-to—and that rain was falling outside. I was covered by a blanket, but I could tell I was shirtless and that some kind of bandaging bound my chest and one shoulder.

"You've got two holes in you, T.G. One in the back where the bullet went in, one in front where it came out. We don't think it hit a lung because you haven't coughed any blood, but you shouldn't move. Does it hurt?"

I managed what was probably a very faint smile. "Like . . .hell . . ." I said weakly. "What . . . happened? The gang . . . ?"

"One hell of a shootout," Sam said. "But four of them got away—"

"Four? But there were five, Sam, five . . ."

Sam looked a little sad. "They didn't all make it, T.G. The little fellow, the one who was first to open up on us. He wasn't as quick to get to his horse as the others. He tried to run but he only hobbled. Luck just wasn't with him. He must have taken four or five slugs, any one of which would have killed him."

I didn't say anything, mostly because I couldn't. Poor Juice. Of all the gang he was undoubtedly the one I had been least close to, but that fact did little to soften the sadness of the moment for me. I guess I had never known anyone who had met such a violent death as that before. The shock of it was pretty great, even then.

Finally, I asked, "The others, Sam. You said they got away?"

Sam nodded. "Unscathed, as best I could tell. One of them was a girl, wasn't she, T.G.? The one that ran to you before one of the others pulled her away and made her get on your horse and ride away with them."

Hazy memories of those moments came back to me, and I was about to answer when I realized that someone else had stepped beneath the lean-to and was now crouching beside Sam.

"How is he?" the man asked.

"Well, he's awake, anyway. T.G., this is Deputy U.S. Marshal Bill Wheeler. He led this posse all the way from El Reno on the trail of that gang you were with."

"Hello, Deputy," I said, weakly extending my right hand.

He said, "I'm sorry about that bullet you took, T.G. We had no idea it was you until Sam here just happened to get a good look at you. To us, it was pure coincidence that this was the gang who took you off that train back in June. I reckon everybody but Sam had just about lost all hope of finding you again."

"Yeah, well, sometimes that's the way things happen," I mumbled.

He and Sam exchanged glances before he went on. "I suppose your brother's already told you—four of them got away clean. Some of us gave them a good chase, but they split up—two going one way, two another—about five miles from here, and it started raining right after that. Looks like they were in luck, after all. No way we'll be able to track them now."

I stared at him. "You did all that and you're already back here?"

He smiled. "We've been back in camp almost an hour, T.G. As a matter of fact, it's half past noon right now."

I stared at Sam.

"You were in shock, T.G.," he explained. "I was plenty worried about you, believe me. It was just lucky there were a couple of men here who knew a thing or two about doctoring, about getting that bleeding stopped and keeping you warm."

I felt terribly weary then. "Am I going to live?"

"Well, we sure hope so!"

For a moment we were all silent. Deputy Wheeler cleared his throat. "We're hoping you can answer some questions for us, T.G. Why they kept you prisoner so long, who they are, where they might have been heading from here. We're especially interested in that last little item, because if we knew, this posse—or some posse, at least—might still have a chance at them."

"How do you know I wasn't one of them?" I asked, trying desperately to decide what I should and should not say. "They told me that's what you would think. After all this time, they said you wouldn't believe I was only their prisoner. They said you would think I had become one of them."

Once again the two men exchanged glances. It was Sam who said, "Wheeler knows you're no outlaw, T.G. Hell, *I* know it. If nothing else, you were unarmed when we found you, you weren't seen with them when the holdup occurred, and you didn't have a dime of that bank money on you when you were shot. We know they had already made their split because the one who was killed had almost two thousand dollars in his money belt."

And I had over eight hundred in my bedroll, I thought. *On that horse Janie rode away on! My cut! But for the grace of God, you'd have found that, too!*

I guess I didn't look very good just then, for Deputy Wheeler said, "We're tiring him, Sam. We can talk about it later on, or even tomorrow. Excuse me, will you, T.G.? We also have a couple of posse members who were wounded. I guess I should be looking in on them, too. You get some rest, you hear?"

He straightened to leave, but I wasn't ready to let him go. "Deputy," I said. "I think I can explain well enough why they kept me prisoner so long. I can also tell you the names they used, but I don't think that will be of much help to you because I'm confident they were only aliases. As for where they were going, well, they weren't very high on letting me know much about their plans, but if it'll help any at all I did overhear them talking once about Canada. They were going to pull this one last job, throw off whatever pursuers they had by faking a run south or west, and then go another way altogether to get out of the country. Canada sure was the only place like that I ever heard them talk about."

That business about Canada wasn't the only lie I was going to have to sleep peacefully with for the rest of my life. Late that afternoon, I told several others to the deputy marshal and Sam. Actually, it was a concoction composed about equally of lies, half lies, and truths. I was honest enough about how I came to be taken prisoner in the first place and to some degree the business about the Dalton masquerade and how my knowledge in that area was why the gang would not let me go. I gave them a vague description of the time we had spent in the Triangle, but left out any mention of having been chased out of there by a posse. Sam and Bill exchanged glances at this but did not say a word. I told them about our hideout on the North Canadian and described accurately where we had camped prior to the El Reno robbery. Beyond those things, however, I omitted whatever I thought I could get away with and made up anything and everything I could to steer them away from, rather than toward, the gang members' true identity and destination.

I invented names for each of the gang—except poor Juice, who I didn't think that would help much now anyway—and I told how I was tied up a lot and never allowed to wander around without someone's gun on me. I told how I was tied to a tree and left under the girl's guard—I called her Rose—while the other four went off to hold up the El Reno bank. I told truthfully about the time I had almost got away and invented at least a couple of other foiled attempts. I thought it out as well as I could and tried not to get trapped in any of my lies. The time or two I was nearly caught in one, I begged their understanding of my current condition, for my memory was confused by that, of course.

I never was sure how fully they believed me. They did not seem suspicious, although there were a few times when I received some pretty quizzical glances. After Wheeler was gone, I was quick to learn that Sam had a question or two of his own that he had reserved for just the two of us to discuss.

"While you were unconscious this morning, you kept moaning a name. No one other than myself heard you, but it certainly wasn't one of the names you gave us or one I ever heard you say before."

I gave him a wary look. "Oh?"

"Someone named Janie. Over and over again, you asked for Janie. Who is Janie, T.G.?"

I looked at my brother Sam, who I hadn't lied to in years before that day, and said, "Janie was just someone I used to know, Sam. Someday when I feel a little more up to it, maybe I'll tell you about her."

For quite a long moment he studied me. "Okay, T.G. But just one more thing . . ." He went on to relate his and the posse's side of the story about that time they had almost captured a gang of outlaws in the Triangle in July. "Are you sure that wasn't your gang, T.G.? You weren't with the bunch we almost caught?"

I met his gaze without batting an eye. "No, Sam. That wasn't us. We were in the Triangle for a spell, but we never saw any posses."

He sighed as he rose. "Well, I guess I should leave you alone now for a spell. We've made you labor a lot here with all of these questions. Tomorrow we're hoping to get you and those other two fellows on the road to a doctor. You can't ride, but it's stopped raining now and Deputy Wheeler has sent some men to see if they can locate a wagon and a team. Try to rest. If you need anything, I won't be far away."

"Sam," I called to him before he could be gone. "Just promise me one thing, will you?"

He turned back. "Sure, T.G. What's that?"

"If I talk any more in my sleep, you wake me up and stop me, okay?"

They found a couple of Caddo Indians who had a team and wagon about five miles north of Deer Creek. The Indians wouldn't let them take the wagon but agreed to hire out to drive it to El Reno, with me, the two wounded possemen, and Juice's body in back. The rest of the posse, including Sam, decided to return there also. They saw no hope now of regaining the trail of the gang, although Deputy Wheeler was restless to start firing off telegrams to other lawmen who could be on the lookout for them between Oklahoma and Canada.

They loaded up as comfortably as they could and we were off shortly after sunup. Of the two men in the wagon with me, one was wounded in the leg and seemed in the least serious condition of the three of us. The other man was gutshot and far worse off than I was. No one gave him much chance of making it, and the poor fellow was suffering horribly. Sam kept me company off and on by riding alongside the wagon, and when he wasn't there I visited with the fellow with the leg wound. We mostly occupied ourselves by complaining about the endless jolts and bumps of the ride and the discomfort and even pain they caused. It made us feel a little better, all the complaining.

Sam didn't ask me any more questions about the gang or my experiences with them, and when along about three o'clock the man with the stomach wound died, the remaining two of us wounded quit complaining about the ride. That we would go the rest of the way with two corpses beside us was reminder enough that we should just be thankful we were still alive.

CHAPTER 20

IN a perfectly austere little second-story El Reno hotel room, I slept in a bed for the first time since I was at the gang's cabin in the Triangle country. I also had my first well-rounded meal in weeks: steak, potatoes, hot biscuits, fresh butter, blackberry jam, and coffee, all brought up from a restaurant next door.

I was also the recipient of substantial attention. First, a kindly old doctor checked out my wounds, bathed, disinfected and redressed them, and pronounced me a likely survivor. Next came Bill Wheeler and a second deputy U.S. marshal, named Simpson, wanting to ask me more questions about the gang. I tried hard to keep my answers consistent with the things I had said before and even secretly prided myself in some of my inventions, especially the "aliases" I had given the gang.

I guess the two law officers were more or less satisfied when they left, for Bill Wheeler told me, "Thanks, T.G. I reckon you've helped us about all you can, although we're probably not the last who will be wanting to hear your story." He paused. "You know you're quite an attraction around here just now. There must be half a dozen newspapermen hanging around just waiting for their chance at you, and more to come after them. And the minute you step out of this hotel, whenever that happens, every Tom, Dick, and Harry on the street is liable to want to talk to you."

When they were gone, Sam laughed at the dourly quizzical look I gave him. "Your experience with that outlaw gang has actually made something of a folk hero of you, T.G."

I only stared at him. I didn't want to be a folk hero; I didn't want any attention; I only wanted out of El Reno and Oklahoma, away from the memories of it. I wanted to forget. I didn't even want to think about it anymore.

Sam said, "I wired Ma soon after we got here. I told her I figured it would be a couple of weeks before you could ride a train home to Missouri. The doc says ten days maybe, if you're a quick mender."

I considered this. Of course I wanted to see Ma and the others again. I had no intention of doing anything else. But somehow going back to Missouri did not excite me very much.

I was curious about something else, however. "How do we pay for all of this, Sam? The hotel room, our train tickets home, our food?"

He wouldn't really tell me, only that it was taken care of and that I needn't worry about it. I suspected every cent the family could pull together was being spent. But I took his advice and let it drop. I was tired and weak and in some pain, and I didn't need anything extra to worry about just then, anyway.

I lay there for three more days, mostly watching Sam—who slept on a cot in one corner of the room—bring in food or carry out my bedpan or stand at the door and tell newspapermen and others that I still wasn't up to talking to them; I watched Sam and did too much thinking . . . far too much thinking . . . almost solely about Janie.

I just could not deal with having lost her. I recalled Clyde having warned us that things might go wrong. Naturally he hadn't foreseen the exact circumstances, but he had seemed to know that something might. Possibly he even saw it as best for everyone. I guess I could almost understand that—from his point of view.

But that did not make dealing with the fact any easier. In my less reasonable moments, I was hurt and even angry that they could just go off and leave me for good—which I was sure was exactly what they had done. Why would Janie let them do that? Did she think I was dead or something? And in what manner had the four of them split up? Deputy Wheeler had said they went two each way. Surely Janie had stayed with Clyde, but where were they now? Had they seen no newspapers proclaiming my rescue and probable survival? It sure would seem strange if they hadn't, the way Clyde liked to read newspapers and all. . . .

Two more days passed. I was up and walking around the room, and my doctor was telling Sam how amazed he was at my progress.

"Spending time with those outlaws must have toughened him up like one of them," he marveled. "You keep an eye on him, you hear, else he may decide to just get up and walk out of here."

I overheard this when I wasn't supposed to, and was not surprised. I was still very sore, and I knew well enough that my wound still had a lot of healing to do. But I felt my strength coming back much more rapidly than I had expected, and I knew that was what the doctor was referring to. Good food and plenty of rest had no doubt contributed much to that.

Two days later Sam came in with our noon meal from the restaurant and said, "Some of those newspaper fellows finally gave up and left, but there are still half a dozen of them here and new ones keep showing up. I think you're finally going to have to talk to them, T.G."

I sighed. I had been putting that off, hoping they would *all* go away. But I could see that some people just aren't so easily discouraged. "Just let me finish lunch," I said. "And bring them in all at once. I don't think I'd be up to entertaining them one at a time."

Sam studied me. "This business with the outlaws sure isn't something you like to talk about, is it, T.G.?"

I only shrugged.

My brother's eyes narrowed perceptively. "Is it the girl, T.G.? The one you call Rose—or is it whoever this Janie is? You still call that name out in your sleep, you know."

I wagged my head slowly. "Trust me, Sam. Soon enough, when things are more right for the telling, I'll unload the whole thing on you. But not yet; just don't press me for it yet."

For a long several moments he just looked at me. "Okay, T.G. I'll be patient about that. But you better be on your toes with those newspaper fellows. I figure whatever it is you're holding back is probably just the kind of thing they'd give their right arms to know!"

Five newspapermen slipped through the door with surprising hesitance, possibly because of the temporary invalid they expected to encounter there. I sat on the edge of my bed, spoiling the role somewhat but quick enough of mind to put on my weakest possible appearance under the circumstances.

They introduced themselves to me, all save one representing Oklahoma or Indian Territory newspapers, and that one claiming to be from Kansas. Perhaps because of that and the fact that he seemed much older, the Kansan caught my attention more than any of the others. He was of medium height and only moderately husky of build, had flowing gray hair, a thick gray beard, deeply sun-tanned features, and very blue eyes. He even looked vaguely familiar to me, but I could not for the life of me place him as anyone I knew. Like the others, he carried a small note pad and wrote constantly in it as I responded to questions. Strangely, however, he never asked me anything, and when he had spoken to introduce himself it was with an exceptionally high-pitched voice of very uneven cadence.

As Sam had predicted, these fellows wanted to know all about my experiences with the outlaws, and were especially interested in the details of my day-to-day existence with them. Once again, I was careful not to create conflict with any of the testimony I had given to the lawmen earlier, and I found myself almost having fun telling those reporters all kinds of little inside tidbits, many of which never happened. At least a couple of times I caught the gray-bearded one — he called himself Charles McCombs — smiling faintly as I talked, almost as if he knew a yarn when he heard one. Still, he did nothing to challenge me and seemed satisfied to just write down answers given to the questions of his peers.

"It must have been terrible to sleep every night bound hand and foot," one of them commented toward the end of the interview.

"It took a half hour every morning just to work the cramps out," I replied dryly.

"And the girl, Rose — you say she was the sister of one of them?"

I nodded warily, having told them this pretty plainly the first time, I thought.

"There wasn't any . . . I mean, she wasn't the, uh, how should I say, lover — yes, lover — of one or more of them?"

I contained my ire at this, but just barely. "Her brother would have killed any of them that so much as looked at her that way," I told him coolly. "She wasn't that kind of girl, anyway. Do you think that just being an outlaw also makes her immoral?"

"Oh," he said, looking somewhat askance at the rebuke. "I see . . ."

It was then that Sam, who had stood nearby throughout, said, "I think my brother is growing tired now, gentlemen. He usually rests about this time. If you don't mind . . ."

They were polite about it, and presently allowed themselves to be herded toward the door. Only the man with the gray beard lagged behind. He sidled past the others and over to me on the bed.

"I just wanted to shake your hand once more," he said in that peculiarly high-pitched voice of his. "Your story has, uh, interested me much more than you probably know."

He leaned forward as our hands met and I suffered two very stunning surprises at the same time. One, from his palm to mine passed a very carefully folded scrap of paper; two, at close range, those blue eyes suddenly became a lot more than just vaguely familiar, and from within his whiskers, his smile for the first time revealed that he had buck teeth.

While my eyes must have fairly bugged and whatever I might have said lodged somewhere deep in my throat, he whispered in an entirely different voice, "Read that and don't let anyone else see it, you hear?"

And then I watched as an almost perfectly disguised Clyde Crosby turned and walked calmly past my brother Sam and out of the room.

I managed to tuck the scrap of paper beneath my bed covers before Sam could see it, then spent a restless hour waiting until he grew bored with talking to me and decided to out for some fresh air on the street. The moment the door closed behind him, I reached for the note Clyde had given me.

Unfolded, it was a larger piece of paper than I had at first realized. My fingers shook as I began to decipher Cyde's somewhat clumsy and not very literate scrawl:

t.g.,

j. and i r here undr disgise. we r registrd in this hotell as man and wif. we are 2 doors down the hall frum yurs. k. and b. went on to the plase we tawked about in that part of the country yu no wher. we will be leeving here on the midnite southbownd tonite on our way to meet them ther as pland.

we saw in a newspapr in texas about wher they had yu and tuk the next train here. if yu r up to it and stil want to go with us find a way to be at the train befor midnite and dont let enyone no about it.

c.c.

p.s. j. wudnt go on unles we at leest made sur yur ok. we have 835 dolars that is yurs to giv to yu ether way.

The trembling in my hands would not stop as I came to a much neater and more learned script than Clyde's:

T.G.,

> *Please don't feel that you must go with us, for I will understand. I love you very much and I know you love me. But I know that things may be different for y ou now that you are back among law-abiding people. Besides, you are wounded and must not do anything that will threaten your recovery.*
>
> *Forgive me that I just couldn't go off without seeing you one more time.*

I love you,
J.

I read it over and over, stopping only when the lump in my throat grew so big I thought I would choke on it.

I told Sam after supper, "I just feel like these walls are closing in on me here. I don't remember ever being in one room so long."

"You've never been laid up like this before, T.G.," Sam said, stacking plates and coffee cups on a tray to be taken back to the restaurant.

"I'm mending faster than expected," I reminded him. "The doc said so himself. I figure I oughta be up to a little walk around outside by now."

Sam thought about it. "Well, I dunno . . ."

"Is there anybody still hanging around outside the room?"

He shook his head. "Not anymore. For the first few days, Bill Wheeler kept a couple of guards out there—I guess mostly just in case members of the gang came back to stop you from talking—but they're gone now. And I think those newspaper fellows have all cleared out, except that fellow McCombs and his wife. I saw them coming into the restaurant for supper just as I was leaving a bit ago . . ."

I felt my pulse quicken at this and thought not for the first time what a reckless thing Clyde and Janie were doing. I still almost could not believe that they were there. . . .

"I suppose you could go with me to take these things back," Sam finally said, indicating the tray. "Just let me help you get your shirt and boots on and we'll go."

We entered an empty hallway outside the room and started down the one flight of stairs. I had been carried up these stairs when I had first arrived and had not noticed how steep they were. Nonetheless, I had no problem going down and was pleased that I did not feel light-headed or anything.

We encountered only a couple of people in the tiny lobby of the hotel, one of which was the night clerk, who said hello to Sam and only looked curiously at me. I guess he wasn't sure if I was the local "folk hero" or not, and it suited me just fine that he didn't ask.

Outside, it was dark and what street lamps there were did little to illuminate the walk between the hotel and the restaurant. I was a little disoriented, and so I asked Sam as we went, "Where's the train station from here?"

He pointed toward a nearby street corner. "At the end of that street. We came right by it when we brought you into town in that wagon. Why? Are you getting anxious to be around trains again? You still have that old love for them, T.G.?"

I shrugged and lied, "Yeah, I guess."

"How do you feel?" he asked as we entered the front door of the restaurant and headed for the kitchen.

"Fine," I said, looking around at the half dozen customers still left there. Then I stopped in my tracks. I know Sam saw them as soon as I did, sitting in a corner booth off to themselves and apparently just finishing their meal. I wouldn't have immediately recognized Janie —her disguise was that good—but I already knew what Clyde's looked like. It was them, no question about it.

Sam only said, "Go on over and say hello to Mr. and Mrs. McCombs if you like. I'll take the tray on to the kitchen."

CHAPTER 21

JANIE wore a long-sleeved, high-necked green dress with lace at the ends of the sleeves and at the neck. She also wore a hat with a barely translucent veil that at least half hid her face. Her hair, what showed of it beneath her hat, was short and gray. Only a very close inspection would have revealed that she was anything but a woman three times her real age.

"You're both crazy, you know that?" I said in a voice too low for anyone else to hear as I shook hands with Clyde and was ostensibly introduced to Janie.

"Are you all right, T.G.?" Janie asked almost immediately. "Your wound—are you in pain?"

"He's fine, Janie," Clyde said impatiently. "Look at him. Now come on, T.G., pull up a chair before your brother gets back."

I did as he said and sat down. "Where on earth did you get the disguises? The beard, the gray hair, the clothes?"

Clyde smiled. "Pretty good, don't you think? We, uh, just happened to acquire a pair of matched gray horses in Cheyenne country and luckily still had them when we learned about you and decided to come back." He stroked his beard lightly. "Clipped every hair of this and our wigs from those old ponies' manes and tails, we did. Tedious work, T.G., damned tedious. And the damned glue itches like hell, let me tell you."

I looked at Janie. "The dress is beautiful. It's only the second time I've seen you in one."

She said softly, "We bought this one and Clyde's suit in Texas. Aren't you proud of us for not getting them some other way? That other old thing I once wore would never have done for this purpose."

I didn't wholly agree. "That 'other old thing' was the first dress I ever saw you in, Janie. Because of that, I think I'll always prefer it over all others. I just thought you were so beautiful, so—"

Clyde was quickly impatient with this. "Come on, T.G., drop that stuff. We haven't got time for it now. Tell us if you're going with us. Hurry, for we have to know tonight."

I never took my eyes off Janie. "I want to—God, how I want to. But it's not that simple. You knew that when you wrote that note. You—"

Janie put a hand on mine. "Yes, T.G., I did know. I'm dying inside because of it, but I *did* know. I knew even when we decided to come here, but I was just so worried about you. I just had to know for certain that you were all right."

I switched my gaze to her brother. "I was wrong, Clyde; I could never really be an outlaw. I couldn't go on living on the run the way you do, and I want no more of robbing banks, trains, or anything else. That little bank you robbed here in El Reno—did you know it may be forced into liquidation because of the money it lost? It's true. A deputy U.S. marshal told me so just the other day. No, I can't do like that. I'm already implicated enough, for you already know of the lies I've told to protect you. Even my brother doesn't know the truth. I'll go on telling the lies, too; I owe you that, and I'll never forget that you came back for me the way you did. But if I go with you now— whether I'm an outlaw at heart or not—I'll be one in fact, nevertheless. And Clyde, don't think I'm fooled by your plans to give it up. I know you think that's what you'll do, but it's not true. This stuff is in your blood. There'll always be one more time until you're caught." I turned back to Janie. "You see that, don't you? You know what I'm saying is true."

I could just glimpse the straight set of her mouth beneath her veil —and that only for an instant before she lowered her head. But that one brief look was all that was needed. She understood well enough.

Clyde just looked sad. "You know, you're a pretty keen pair of kids. But it just seems there ought to be some way—"

Something he had spotted over my shoulder caused him to stop then. I turned to see Sam striding our way.

"That cook back there sure loves to talk," he said as he came to stand beside me. "Sometimes I almost can't get away from him."

I rose from my chair a bit awkwardly. "Sam, you've met Mr. McCombs. This is his . . . wife . . . er, I guess I didn't catch the first name . . ."

Janie never hesitated. "Julia," she said softly. "It's Julia."

Sam sort of bowed and said, "Pleasedtomeetcha." Then he switched his gaze to Clyde. "Will you folks be staying in El Reno long?"

Clyde assumed the high-pitched voice of Charles McCombs. "Well, no, in fact. We plan to be on the first train home tomorrow."

"Back to Kansas," Sam mused, nodding. "Well, that should be about the first thing after daylight tomorrow, which is when the first Rock Island northbound comes through, if I'm not mistaken."

Clyde seemed momentarily lost in thought. "What's that? Oh, yes. that'll be it, I reckon. First thing tomorrow."

Nobody said anything for a few seconds and finally Sam looked at me. "Well, I suppose we should be going, T.G. I'd rather you didn't overdo things first time out of your room. Mr. and Mrs. McCombs, I'm sure T.G. and I both wish you the best on your trip home."

I didn't know what to say. My visit with Clyde and Janie— especially Janie—was being cut far too short and there was nothing I could do about it without running the risk of giving them away.

I could only mumble a not very hopeful, "Possibly I'll see you both again before you leave."

Clyde's expression was still thoughtful. "It'll be very early tomorrow. But yes, it would be good to see you before then. Yes, it would."

Because of the veil, I couldn't see Janie's eyes or tell much about her expression, only that her lips trembled the moment before she looked down and away from me. It was the hardest thing I believe I ever had to do to follow Sam away from there then.

"The woman, Mrs. McCombs," my brother said as we negotiated the stairs back up to our room. "I wonder why she wears that veil. I mean, doesn't that seem strange to you, T.G.?"

I made as if the stairs were tiring me, and only said, "I dunno. Maybe she's got a scar on her face. . . . Hell, how should *I* know something like that?"

I just couldn't let it end that way. I didn't know yet what I was going to do otherwise, but I knew I had to see Janie again.

I considered very seriously telling Sam all about it, thinking to enlist his help in deciding what I should do. But could I be sure he would understand? He might even try to stop me. No way I could chance that. I could not go to Sam for help.

Somehow, though, my brother was slow to want to go to bed that night. We stayed up until almost nine-thirty, just talking—mostly Sam doing the talking about things back home, while I yawned and pretended weariness and wished to God he'd at least catch the disease if not the hint.

Finally he did yield to one or the other. "You want me to help you off with your boots and shirt?" he asked from his cot in the corner where he struggled to remove one of his own boots.

"Naw," I said, fingering my shirt buttons with one hand. "I figure I oughta be able to do for myself by now."

"You want me to get the lamp?"

"No, I'll get it. Go ahead."

Sam crawled into bed as I went over and blew out the lamp. I came back in the dark to my bed, then sat down, ostensibly to finish undressing. I thumped the floor with the heel of one boot, as if I had actually removed it and let it fall. About a minute later, I thumped the floor again. Actually, I was busy rebuttoning my shirt. I pulled the covers back and laid down on my bed, still fully clothed.

"Sleep well," Sam said.

"Aim to," I lied like a trooper.

I didn't know for certain how difficult it was going to be to get away with, but I was determined to slip out of the room the minute I was sure Sam was fast asleep.

The only way I was going to know about that was if Sam snored. Sometimes he slept more lightly than at other times. When he slept lightly, he didn't snore and the least noise would wake him up. When he slept soundly, he snored and six horses in the room probably wouldn't rouse him.

For the longest time the only noises he made were those of tossings and turnings. I lay as still as I could, hoping not to disturb him but convinced that he was not yet really asleep. I grew nervous. I had looked at my pocket watch before blowing out the lamp and was certain that no less than thirty minutes had elapsed since that time. That would make it shortly past ten. If Clyde and Janie were going to make a midnight train, they would leave their room down the hall probably no later than eleven-fifteen or so. I still had plenty of time if Sam would only go ahead and get to sleep.

I don't know how it happened, for I should have been anything but sleepy myself. I guess I was pretty tired and just didn't realize it.

I caught myself dozing only once and opened my eyes wide in an effort to combat drowsiness. It didn't work very well, for the next thing I knew I was coming awake with a start and the icy fear that I had slept right past midnight.

Sam wasn't snoring, but I no longer had the luxury of caring about that. I rose and went straight for the door, opened it, and stepped into the hallway. The lamps that ordinarily illuminated that area early in the evening had already been blown out, probably by the night clerk from downstairs.

The only light was at the head of the stairs and that coming from the lobby below. Quickly I moved over to the stairs and drew out my watch. I could just make out the hands; it was eleven-forty-five.

With a terrible something clutching at my insides, I felt my way to the second door past Sam's and mine. I knocked lightly and waited. There was no answer. I tried the latch and found it unlocked. The room was darkened, and I was not surprised.

Nevertheless, I called softly, "Janie? Clyde?"

There was no answer. Only the barest light came through an open window. I could just make out two empty beds, on opposite sides of the room, and possibly a dresser. With a sinking sensation, I realized that not only were Janie and Clyde gone, but that the time for the midnight southbound's departure was growing painfully near.

I whirled back toward the hallway, wondering which way to go. There were of course the stairs leading to the first floor lobby, but I was pretty sure I had seen a door at the other end of the hallway when Sam and I had gone down earlier. If I was right, that door could only lead to the outside of the building, and being on the second floor, it could only lead to a stairway to the back alley.

Because I didn't really want to have to pass by the night clerk, I chose to try that door at the end of the hall. It was latched from the inside—a fact easily remedied—and I quickly found that I was right about the outer stairway and the alley.

With hardly a thought for my weakened condition, I descended the stairs and made my way around the corner of the building toward the street. Once there, I quickly oriented myself in the direction Sam had told me I would have to go to reach the train station. There was no one on the street at that hour and the street lamps were dim. I knew I wasn't up to running yet, but the desperation inside me was so great I didn't care. I ran anyway. I heard the whistle of what I presumed was the midnight southbound coming from the station as I ran.

The train sat there, engine hissing steam in front of its tender, and express car and baggage car, a single coach, a Pullman sleeper, and a caboose. The darkened platform was empty except for the conductor clutching a lantern and one other man who looked about to board. They stood at the rear steps of the sleeper.

I was very much out of breath, nearing exhaustion, by the time I reached the platform, and my shoulder throbbed from the shock of each step I had taken. The man who had been standing with the conductor had already boarded and the conductor was looking toward the engine and away from me. He was just in the process of raising his lantern to wave a signal to the engine crew when he must have heard me clomping up behind him.

I know he was startled—he may even have been briefly frightened—by the stumbling, half-coherent apparition that burst upon him. For certain he did not know what to make of me, and I was too out of breath to effectively explain.

"A man . . . a woman . . . have they already . . . ?"

He grabbed me as much to keep me from going any farther as to keep me from falling, which wasn't too unlikely as I was practically at the point of collapse. He held his lantern aloft, almost in my face.

"What's the matter with you, man? Are you drunk?"

I heard the long, slow blast of the engineer's whistle signaling his preparedness to pull out. Steam hissed up front. I grew desperate.

"An older man," I huffed. "Gray beard . . . a woman about the same age with him . . . did they . . . board?"

He eyed me in a suspicious manner and continued to hold the lantern in my face. "Well, yes, there was such a couple. Them and a fellow who just boarded who is bound for Chickasaw to visit a dying relative. The older couple got on over ten minutes ago. But look here, young fellow, this train is about to be behind schedule as it is. Do you intend to board? Do you have a ticket?"

I stared at him. "No . . . but I . . . I mean . . ." I just could not get my breath. I tried to see if I could catch a glimpse of anyone through the rear few windows of the Pullman, but all were curtained for the night. The co..ductor continued to block my way.

For the barest instant I was distracted by what I thought was movement at the steps on the other end of the sleeper. But the only light there came indirectly from a few uncurtained coach windows and what dim few rays strayed from the doorway of the station building across the platform. And that fool conductor persisted in holding his lantern high, all but blinding me and making it impossible for me to see well beyond him.

Up the track, the hissing of steam suddenly stopped. I then heard the first slow chuff of the engine as the locomotive's drive wheels began to turn, followed quickly by the clank of couplings engaging.

"Look," the conductor said. "I'm sorry. This train is on the roll and if you're not boarding you'll have to step back. Do it, will you?"

Already the car was moving. The conductor actually had to leap to make it aboard. I tried to follow suit but tripped and fell face forward on the platform, just barely managing to break my fall with my hands as I went down. For a moment, the pain in my left shoulder was blinding. But then I realized that the caboose was passing me, its wheels clanking where each set of rails met. I struggled to my feet just in time to watch the rear of the car go past but not in time to catch the step railing. I tried to run, but my legs were weak and I stumbled and fell again. All I could do was watch the lights of the caboose as the train moved off into the night, chuffing, clanking, whistling, gaining speed. . . .

I struggled to regain my feet, but this time with nothing to do but stand there and watch the train move away. I couldn't stop it; I couldn't catch it. It was gone. My heart felt like lead inside my chest, and shameless tears started to rise as I realized that Janie and Clyde were gone with the train.

But then I thought I saw something on the platform not a sleepers car length away from me. Someone standing there. A slender figure, ghost-like. A voice came dimly through to me, someone saying my name. The figure wore a dress, and the voice was both familiar and sweet and feminine. But she only stood there with a very small suitcase at her feet, as if frozen to the spot, and I thought it really couldn't be, that she truly was only an apparition.

But then she picked up the suitcase and started my way, and somehow I knew she was real.

"Janie? Oh God, *Janie!*"

Later, I would not even remember striding to meet her, but in seconds she was in my arms, sobbing and putting her face up to mine for me to kiss away the tears.

"Janie . . . how did you . . . ? I thought you were on the train. How on earth did you . . . ?"

My voice cracked as I spoke, but hers was barely audible. "Clyde and I boarded together. All the other passengers were asleep. The train was stopped for over ten minutes. I changed dresses and left my gray wig and veil behind the curtains of my berth. I left Clyde to continue on with the train. I—I got off at the opposite end of the sleeper from where the conductor had been standing, hoping to look like a passenger who had planned to stop here all along . . ."

I stepped back to look at her. In lieu of the disguise and the green dress, she wore the blue dress I had told her would always be a favorite of mine.

She went on, "Oh, T.G., I just couldn't leave you! I was afraid you wouldn't want me to stay, but Clyde . . . Clyde actually insisted on it. He said you were right about him and the gang—they will probably be outlaws to the end. He said I'd be a fool to trade you for them. He said no one would know me here, and that we should be able to invent some kind of story to explain who I am. He told me I had to make a permanent break with the gang now, while I had a chance. When I finally agreed, I also made him take both of our shares of the bank loot. Oh, T.G., I was so afraid you wouldn't come. That this would never work. Did I do wrong?"

I drew her to me once more. "No, Janie. You did anything but wrong. You had more guts than I did, is all. And Clyde, give him credit, had more good sense. Thank God for that!"

Even so, some uncertainty remained. "We still have to think of exactly what we're going to tell people, T.G. Your brother, especially. How are we going to explain *me* to him?"

I was too overwhelmed with emotion to let that bother me even a whit. "We'll think of something," I promised. "Don't you worry about that. We'll think of something."

Suddenly I heard a footstep behind me and someone put a hand on my shoulder. I turned to see who I figured must be the night station attendant for the Rock Island.

"Is there something I can do for you folks? Did someone miss the train? I don't recall selling either of you a ticket. There's another southbound coming through tomorrow, though. It won't be the end of the world that you missed this one . . ."

I almost laughed as I said, "No. Oh, no. My friend is getting off here, not on. We're fine, we really are."

And then I heard more footsteps, and I was shocked to see my brother Sam come striding across the platform to stop before us.

For a moment Sam just stood there and stared at Janie and me, waiting, I guess, for the attendant to disappear back inside the station.

Finally he said, "I reckon you weren't quiet enough when you snuck away from your bed, little brother. But you got away before I could get dressed and follow you. Then I heard the train whistle and remembered you asking where the station was. It was only a gamble, but I thought I might find you here."

I couldn't think of anything to say. I just stared back at him.

He was looking at Janie. "Well, T.G., one thing about it, you never were short on surprises. Aren't you going to tell me who your friend is?"

When I finally found my voice, I said, "Somehow I don't think you're going to be surprised, Sam. This is Janie. She is the one you've been asking about for the past two weeks, after every time I talked in my sleep. Janie, my brother Sam."

He just stood there nodding, waiting. I think he knew he had met her before, earlier that very evening. I think my brother was beginning to put an awful lot together very quickly.

Nonetheless, I said, "It's a pretty complicated story, Sam. It'll take some patient listening on your part and a lot of trust on ours. I only hope you'll be willing to understand and that you'll want to help us when you've heard."

His response to this was decidedly stern. "I've been helping you all your life, little brother. I don't know why I'd stop now. Just make your story the truth this time, that's all I ask."

And then my good and faithful brother, who I should have trusted so much more so much sooner, smiled down at Janie, whose tears still glistened on her cheeks, and said, "I think it's going to be a real privilege to get to know you, girl. And don't worry. Whatever the problems are, I'm sure we'll work them out somehow. I think you can count on that."

We started back toward the hotel together, and behind us the train whistle grew distant and somewhat forlorn to our ears. Only once did Janie stop to look back, a final farewell to her brother, I knew.

I also looked back, but for only that one sad-happy moment. My summer with outlaws was over, but my life with Janie was only just begun.